1937- Amelia Earhart
giving rise to one of hist

When searchers believe they have found the location of Earhart's crash-landing, Navy SEALs Dane Maddock and Bones Bonebrake are sent on a covert mission to locate Earhart's crashed Electra aircraft and recover its contents. But nothing is ever easy for Dane and Bones. They soon find themselves facing off against mercenary forces, deadly creatures, and nature itself. Join Dane and Bones on another action-packed adventure as they head out in search of Electra!

Praise for the Dane Maddock Adventures

"Another rip-roaring thrill ride of an adventure for Dane and Bones! Thriller fans won't want to miss!" –Joseph Nassise, international bestselling author of *The Templar Chronicles.*

"Call in sick tomorrow, it's going to be a late night! Shades of Jurassic Park set against a Russian special forces backdrop with old friends Dane and Bones at it again--Dead Ice is dead on!" -Rick Chesler, author of *Solar Island* and *Wired Kingdom*

"Dane and Bones…. Together they're unstoppable. Rip roaring action from start to finish. Wit and humor throughout. Just one question – how soon until the next one? Because I can't wait." -Graham Brown, author of *Shadows of the Midnight Sun*

"Packs in the fist fights, cipher cracking and ancient secrets that all action adventure lovers will enjoy."- J.F. Penn, author of the *ARKANE* thrillers.

"Ancient cave paintings? Cities of gold? Secret scrolls? Sign me up! Cibola is a twisty tale of adventure and intrigue that never lets up and never lets go!" –Robert Masello, author of *Bestiary* and *Blood and Ice*

ELECTRA

A Dane and Bones Origins Story

DAVID WOOD
RICK CHESLER

Gryphonwood

Gryphonwood Press

ELECTRA- A DANE AND BONES ORIGINS
STORY.

Published by Gryphonwood Press
www.gryphonwoodpress.com

Edited by Michael Dunne

ISBN-10: 1940095247
ISBN-13: 978-1-940095-24-0

Printed in the United States of America
First printing: August, 2014.

Books by David Wood

Dane Maddock Adventures
Dourado
Cibola
Quest
Icefall
Buccaneer
Atlantis
Ark (forthcoming)

Dane and Bones Origins
Freedom (with Sean Sweeney)
Hell Ship (with Sean Ellis)
Splashdown (with Rick Chesler)
Dead Ice (with Steven Savile)
Liberty (with Edward G. Talbot)
Electra (with Rick Chesler)

The Jade Ihara Adventures
Oracle (with Sean Ellis-forthcoming)
Changeling (with Sean Ellis- forthcoming)

Stand-Alone Works
Into the Woods (with David S. Wood)
Callsign: Queen (with Jeremy Robinson)
Dark Rite (with Alan Baxter)
The Zombie-Driven Life
Arena of Souls
You Suck

Writing as David Debord
The Silver Serpent
Keeper of the Mists
The Gates of Iron (forthcoming)
The Impostor Prince (with Ryan A. Span- forthcoming)

Books by Rick Chesler

Tara Shores Thrillers
Wired Kingdom
kiDNApped
Solar Island

OUTCAST Ops Series (with Rick Jones)
Game of Drones
The Poseidon Initiative

Other Works
Jurassic Dead (with David Sakmyster)
Blood Harbor: A Novel of Suspense
Lucifer's Machine (with Steven Savile)
Splashdown (with David Wood)
O.U.T.C.A.S.T. Ops series (with Rick Jones -
forthcoming)

Writing as Jack Douglas
Quake (With Douglas Corleone - forthcoming)

This book is dedicated to all my friends who make up Maddock's Minions. You are the best!

PROLOGUE

July 2, 1937, 8:49 A.M., South Pacific Ocean

What was real and what was a trick of the light? From an altitude of one thousand feet, the shadows of cumulus clouds on the ocean appeared the same as the low-lying island Amelia Earhart was looking for. Her plane was about to crash. Nothing she could do would change that. She needed somewhere to land and somewhere to land fast.

Earhart and her navigator, Fred Noonan, were on the most difficult leg of their journey after having flown two-thirds of the way around the planet in their Lockheed Electra airplane. Earlier that day they had departed Lae, New Guinea en route to tiny Howland Island, where they were to make a refueling stop before traveling on to Honolulu. From there, San Francisco represented the completion of their goal—a circumnavigation of the globe at the equator, piloted by a woman, an almost unimaginable accomplishment.

Things had not gone as planned since Lae, however, and now Earhart was forced to make a choice: she thought that dark patch below and to the right was part of an island—probably not Howland or even nearby Baker, but beggars couldn't be choosers. It offered what looked like enough flat ground on which to try a crash-landing, but if she was wrong she wouldn't be able to regain altitude to try somewhere else.

She smiled to herself in spite of the situation, recalling good times spent with her pilot mentors. "Any landing you can walk away from..." She could hear them laughing across all the miles and all the years. This once humble farm girl, born in America's heartland in 1897, six years before the pivotal Wright brothers' first flight, had come farther than she had ever dreamed, both literally and figuratively.

Now, as the waves of the Pacific rushed up to greet her,

it all came down to this. She squinted through her goggles at the outline below—*there!* A white line indicating breaking waves on a reef. It was real land and not just a cloud shadow. She would at least have a chance. But there was yet another problem.

She needed desperately to communicate with Noonan, who sat ten feet behind her in the cargo area, rather than in the co-pilot's seat, to accommodate his navigation equipment. The combined noise of air rushing into the plane and its twin Pratt & Whitney engines made it very loud, however, making normal conversation impossible. To overcome this, they had devised a crude clothesline system where they clipped a paper with a written message to a clothespin and slid it back and forth on a pulley. In this way they could communicate during the long hours in the air. Right now, though, there was no time for that. But with her engines out, there wasn't as much noise as usual and by shouting she could make herself heard. She craned her neck to face backward and yelled, "Secure the payload, Fred! Secure it now!"

She could just make out his reply. "Okay!"

Earhart quickly glanced to her right and frowned, then focused her full attention on the little island below. Much of it was forested and offered no hope of a real landing. On the far side of the island she picked out a pathetically small strip of sand or crushed coral, and she nosed her plummeting craft toward that.

She was not sure she would be able to reach it.

CHAPTER 1

San Diego, California

"Remember, only one member of your dive team needs to avoid detection for that team to be declared the winners of this exercise!" The U.S. Navy underwater warfare trainer spoke forcefully, almost shouting, as he addressed the two Navy SEALs who stood before him, as well as a dozen others who sat on the dock nearby.

For Navy SEAL Dane Maddock, the statement offered little consolation. He and the SEAL he had been paired with, Uriah "Bones" Bonebrake, would be the last team to attempt the exercise, which so far none of their peers had been able to complete. Maddock stood on a floating dock at the entrance to a military harbor, surveying his surroundings. He squinted against the bright morning sunlight as he focused on their goal: a destroyer ship docked in the harbor about one hundred yards away, a large red flag draped over one side indicating its training target status. The SEALs were supposed to act as enemy combatants infiltrating the harbor, by SCUBA diving through it and sticking a mine on the warship's hull. Maddock felt the pouch on his weight belt that contained the mine to make sure it was fastened securely. Bones also gave his equipment a last-second inspection. Their task would be difficult enough without any gear failures.

"Divers *ready*..."

Their warfare trainer spoke through a megaphone now, alerting those in the vicinity about what was taking place. Maddock sized up their foes—the two opponents whose job it would be to stop the SEALs from placing a mine on the ship. They were superior swimmers, much better than Maddock and Bones, and they always seemed to wear annoyingly cocky grins on their faces. This would be a test for them, too.

"Mark 7 team, *ready...*"

The two bottlenose dolphins circled in their enclosure, an underwater pen with a sliding door which their handler, a marine mammal specialist, now lifted and held open. The United States Navy Marine Mammal Program had been in quiet, low-key operation since the early 1960s, with significant deployments during the Vietnam War and other conflicts. The long-classified program trained dolphins and sea lions to perform useful underwater tasks such as mine detection, the recovery of underwater objects, and, as would be demonstrated in this exercise, the protection of harbors from attacks by scuba divers.

Bones glared at one of the animals as if he could intimidate it. It outweighed him, out-swam him, had additional senses he did not possess, and, depending on whom one asked, was possibly even smarter than him. Unlike the trainers at public dolphin facilities like Sea World who constantly cooed in soothing tones to their charges while wearing brightly colored outfits, this trainer conveyed instructions to his dolphins almost exclusively by hand signals, wore military uniform, and never seemed to offer fish as treats. The dolphins were well-cared for and knew they would be fed well at the end of the day. A word of praise was reward enough.

Maddock, who had been staring at the destroyer, lost in tactical thought, snapped out of it. He flexed his knees in the wetsuit he wore to ward off the chilly water. The suit limited mobility somewhat, but it was important not only to retain body heat in a medium that transferred heat away from the body twenty-five times faster than air, but also to shield their bodies from accidental blows the dolphins might deliver. They could easily kill a man with blunt force, but were trained only to tag the divers by placing a magnetic disc which would deploy a buoy marker when activated. When these yellow markers floated to the surface, Navy officers would then make a decision about how to intercept the potential threat. Maddock observed the dolphin handler closely as he communicated with his mammalian subjects.

"Mark 7 team, set, *go*."

The handler blew two short blasts from his whistle and the pair of cetaceans burst from their pen into the open water of the harbor entrance. They would be given three minutes to swim to the destroyer at the other end of the harbor before the dive team hit the water. Maddock and Bones watched the sleek animals recede into the harbor until they were no longer visible.

"And to think I used to like that show Flipper when I was a kid." Bones shook his head. Of American Indian descent, his six-foot-six frame and muscular build intimidated many a human warrior, but would matter little to the dolphins.

Maddock frowned at his friend and colleague with eyes the shade of a stormy sea. He often found Bones' outgoing demeanor irritated his more reserved personality. It wasn't that long ago that the two had butted heads in BUDS school while training to be SEALs, but gradually they had gotten to know each other through the course of various missions and adventures. Now they had what Maddock considered a good working relationship, although he wished Bones would shut his mouth sometimes.

"Divers: *set*..."

Maddock leaned over to Bones. "Let's stick together." The other teams had operated on the principle that splitting up underwater offered greater odds of success. But to Maddock, it also meant each diver was more exposed, more on their own. It hadn't worked so far. Bones just had time to nod before their warfare trainer spoke once more into his megaphone.

"Go!"

Maddock and Bones slipped into the water of the harbor with barely a ripple at the same time as the marine mammal trainer gave a sustained blast of his whistle.

The clarity of the water left a lot to be desired. They could see perhaps ten feet in front of them and knew that it would only get worse the deeper into the harbor they ventured. The dolphins, meanwhile, depended less on sight and more on their echolocation sense, a kind of natural SONAR that allowed them to "see" objects by pinging them with sound waves generated from their melons. Maddock knew they would have no trouble picking out two human forms.

They reached the muddy bottom at a depth of about twenty feet. Like their fellow SEALs who had already tried and failed, the thinking was that if you were near the bottom, at least the dolphins couldn't profile you from below. Maddock took a bearing from a compass he wore on his wrist and pointed toward the destroyer. They would swim straight toward it. Sneaking along the edges of the harbor, which provided some small measure of shielding, also took more time, thus giving the dolphins more time to detect and tag them. Bones nodded and the two warriors swam at a rapid pace toward their target.

There was little to see except for the flat muddy seabed. Clouds of silt puffed into the water when their fin strokes got too close. Maddock glanced at his dive watch. They'd been swimming hard for two minutes. It wouldn't be long before the marine mammal sentries began sizing them up and closing in. They would swoop in and plant the magnetic buoy on their tanks, as they had been trained. If intimidating physical gestures or movements worked, the other teams would have had success by now.

Maddock pulled on one of Bones' fin tips to gain his attention. The big Indian whirled around. Maddock held up the index finger of each hand and then drew them together, indicating that he and Bones should stick close together. Bones looked around, head on a swivel. When he saw nothing he held his hands up in a *what's up* gesture. Maddock wrote with a pencil on the underwater slate he had clipped to his dive vest.

STAND TANK-TO-TANK AND WALK IN ON BOTTOM

Maddock watched as Bones' eyes narrowed in confusion behind his mask. He was a fast, powerful swimmer, they were making progress toward their goal, and now Maddock wanted to stop and do something weird? At the same time, Bones had been in the field with Maddock enough times to know that he wouldn't propose a tactic he hadn't already thought through.

Bones shrugged, took a last look around and settled into an upright position, fins flat on the bottom. Maddock did the same and backed up to him so that their air tanks each contacted the others' back, severely limiting the amount of exposed metal. Maddock checked his compass, tapped Bones' arm and pointed toward the destroyer.

They proceeded to move across the bottom in a strange kind of crab-walk, their progress slow and plodding. They slowly rotated as they moved, kicking up the mud as they went along, further limiting their visibility. After a couple of minutes of progress, Maddock caught a streak of movement in his peripheral vision. He could no longer see anything there, but he knew it had to be a dolphin, shooting by, making a surveillance pass. He felt a tap on his arm and looked back to see Bones pointing off to their right. He, too, had seen something.

They kept walking across the bottom of the harbor. Maddock glanced at his watch, tracking exercise elapsed time. At least one of the previous teams had been tagged out by now. Two more forms shot past them, closer this time, one on each side of them and moving in opposite directions. They were closing in.

Still, they kept moving, Maddock keeping a close eye on the compass. The going was slow and they didn't need to go anywhere but straight to the target. Had they been swimming, they could have reached the ship by now. But at the same time, more minutes had ticked by, and Maddock knew that by now some of the SEALs on the dock would be surprised that they hadn't seen a yellow marker pop up yet.

Then he felt Bones slip and the big man fell in slow motion toward the bottom, rolling over on one side. Instantly one of the gray marauders homed in, the magnetic buoy tag clenched in its formidable peg-like teeth. Maddock kicked at its snout as it closed in, the dolphin easily avoiding his finned foot with an effortless swerve of its head. He heard a shrill series of staccato clicks and whistles and could only speculate it was a fighter's trash talk.

Or perhaps tactical coordination?

Almost too late, Maddock turned while Bones got to his feet in time to see the other dolphin swimming toward them at ramming speed. Maddock spun, eliciting a muffled grunt from Bones as he slammed his tank into his ribcage. But the dolphin missed, its muscular side careening off Maddock's wetsuit as it rocketed past. Maddock now realized full well what they were up against. There was no way a mid-water swimmer would get past these aquatic sentries, no matter how skilled. His tactic was paying off.

He gripped Bones' shoulder and looked into his eyes when he turned around. *Okay?* Bones held up a thumb and finger in a circle, the universal diver's *okay* sign. They began their slow dance toward the warship once more. Maddock hoped the trail of silt they kicked up might confuse the dolphins' echolocation, causing their pings to bounce back before reaching them. The animals began to circle around them like sharks, moving slower now, studying their quarry, looking for a weakness.

The next time Maddock looked up from his compass he was rewarded with the sight of the dark underbelly of a U.S. Navy destroyer. Perhaps fifteen feet above them and another ten feet away, it represented their objective. The dolphins stayed with them as they passed under its hull into near darkness, the massive ship blotting out the sunlight. They could hear vibrations coming from the war machine, not its propulsion system but various machinery on board as sailors carried out their business in port.

When they were directly under the middle of the hull, the V-shaped part of the ship that was deepest underwater, Maddock signaled to Bones to stop moving. They looked up and saw the metal surface, painted black with antifouling paint, a mere ten feet above them. Maddock unclipped the snaps on his mine pouch.

The dolphins were still right there, chattering

incessantly. They, too, seemed to know that this was the endgame. Maddock was tempted to make a dash for the underbelly of the vessel, but suppressed the urge. They'd come too far to get careless now. He summoned some of the discipline SEALs were known for and forced himself to think. *What would work here?*

The tanks back-to-back was the thing. They had to stay in that formation. He signaled to Bones that they would ascend together in the same orientation. He was relieved to see the Indian simply nod his agreement. He must also be surprised they'd made it this far.

Then the dolphins disappeared and Maddock guessed they were going to the surface to take a breath. Dolphins typically surfaced to breathe every few minutes and they'd been down longer than that.

Now! He widened his eyes at Bones and the two of them began a slow and careful ascent toward the ship's metal underside, spinning slowly in a circle as they neared the spot where they would place a mine. Maddock slipped the heavy disc from his pouch—a ballistically inert training model—and waved it in front of Bone's face, his message clear: *I'll place the mine.*

The combat dolphins were back by the time Maddock was within arm's reach of the metal structure. Very aggressive now, they darted in and nosed around Maddock's and Bones' midsections, seeking access to the scuba tanks. Maddock gripped his own magnetic disc tightly in his hand, waiting for an opening. He didn't want a dolphin to nose it out of his grasp. When he saw both dolphins move to Bones' side, teaming up on him, Maddock made his move.

He thrust an arm up until he felt the mine snap onto the hull with a satisfying *clack*. The LED on the explosive device turned from green to red and began to blink. Maddock knew that it was now transmitting a signal to the training officials that the mine had been triggered.

Although technically they had won the exercise, since a suicide bomber's mission would be complete at this point, not caring if he were caught or killed, Maddock still wanted to reach the surface without being tagged at all, if possible. Extra points. He was glad to see Bones fall into formation by his side and together they awkwardly swam their way out from under the ship. The dolphins still followed them but seemed to have lost some of their fight, perhaps knowing the game had already been won.

Still together as a unit, Maddock and Bones surfaced next to the destroyer. They were still untagged as their heads broke the surface and the first thing Maddock heard was the dolphin trainer's whistle. After a moment, the dorsal fins of their two adversaries were seen slicing the water in the direction of their holding pen on the floating docks.

Looking up at the destroyer, Maddock saw the excited faces of the sailors leaning over the rail, many of them clapping and cheering.

Maddock held his hands up and pantomimed an explosion.

"Gotcha!" he called up to the crew.

"Nice work!"

"Got lucky!" The calls came down.

As a small Zodiac inflatable boat neared Maddock and Bones for pickup, a gruff voice issued over the ship's PA system.

"Maddock, Bonebrake: come on up to the Commander's office. Now!"

CHAPTER 2

"The C.O. wants to see us?" Maddock asked the SEAL driving the inflatable boat as they motored to the destroyer's boarding ladder. The boat operator nodded and gave him a serious look.

"Yes, sir. I brought your rucks so you have your clothes to change into aboard the ship." He nodded to two backpacks on the floor of the boat.

"Thanks." Maddock grabbed them and handed one to Bones, who addressed the boat driver.

"You know anything about why he wants to see us?"

A shake of the head as the driver eased back on the throttle while he approached the destroyer's ladder. "No, sir. Whatever it is, it must be important, though. Succeeding in a training exercise, as impressive as that was, wouldn't normally warrant this. Good luck," he finished, sidling the boat up to the ship.

Once granted permission to board, Maddock and Bones climbed the ladder and stepped onto the deck of the warship. They were greeted by a sailor who asked them to accompany him. He moved off at a brisk pace and they followed him into an inside area where he stopped and opened a door.

"You can change in here. Just leave the wetsuits." He glanced at his watch. Maddock and Bones stepped into the room and emerged a minute later in casual uniform; fatigues and navy blue T-shirts. The sailor led them down the hall until they emerged outside again but beneath the shadow of an overhanging deck. From there they entered a tall structure and began climbing tight, winding flights of stairs. One such ended in a small open area with doorways leading to several rooms. Their escort showed them to one of the doors and opened it for them, extending a hand inside.

"Commander Roberts will see you now."

Maddock and Bones stepped into a small office where a thin, bald man sat behind a desk in full, starched white uniform. He was on a phone saying, "...so send her up...Yes, now!" and hung up as soon as he saw his two SEALS enter.

"Gentlemen, sit down. No time to waste." Maddock and Bones took seats in the two chairs fronting the desk, a nameplate on it reading, Cmdr Stephen Roberts. The commander smiled at the two SEALs.

"Congratulations on blowing up my ship! You can bet this is the only time you'll ever hear me say that."

"Be sure and give the Flipper twins a sardine for me."

The commander smirked at Bones' joke and then grew serious. "Listen up. I've got a mission for you two. It's highly classified. It's deadly serious. It starts today. Are you ready to pay very close attention?"

Maddock and Bones nodded.

"Excellent. Here we go. Downstairs on the helipad is a Sikorsky waiting to take you to San Diego International Airport, where you'll catch a commercial flight." He pushed a pair of travel vouchers across the desk. Maddock opened his first and read the destination.

"Honolulu?"

"Hell, yes!" Bones pumped his fist and began to hula dance, his bulk making his chair squeak. Commander Roberts frowned in his direction and he froze. "Sorry."

"I'm afraid you won't be there long enough to enjoy Mai Tais on Waikiki Beach." Roberts pushed another set of envelopes at them and continued while Maddock and Bones picked them up.

"From there you transfer to another commercial flight to Manila. But your destination is not the Philippines, either." He slid one more set of papers to them.

"Use these last ones at the private air charter counter at Manila International. The pilot will drop you off on a small island in the equatorial South Pacific."

The questioning gazes the commander was greeted with told him Maddock and Bones were ready for him to continue.

"What do you know about Amelia Earhart?"

Maddock frowned and Bones scratched his temple.

"That much?" the commander said after a few seconds of silence. "You'll need to read these reports during your flight over." He passed them each a folder full of documents before continuing. "By the time you reach the island, you should be well-versed in the generally accepted body of knowledge concerning Earhart's final flight."

"She went missing somewhere over the Pacific, in the 1930s on a flight to circumnavigate the globe, correct?" Maddock spoke before he picked up his folder.

"That's right." The commander appeared slightly surprised but quickly moved on. "To be more specific, however, we believe that she went missing at the island you'll be visiting." He held up a hand, forestalling Maddock's exclamation of surprise. "There's a chance of it, anyway. Let me explain."

He unfolded a paper map on his desk and smoothed it over.

"So as you can see here," he said, pointing to a spot on the map, "there's a tremendous amount of open water. A private group calling themselves EARHART, appropriately enough—an acronym for Early Aviation Research and Historic Aircraft Recovery Team, although they are unaffiliated with the family—has recently announced that they may have found Amelia Earhart's airplane off the coast of *this* island in scuba-accessible depths." He stabbed the chart with the point of a pencil.

"Private group? So it's not a military operation?" Bones asked, implying the obvious question. *So what are we doing here?*

"Yes, private group. It's not a military operation for *them*." Roberts looked up from the chart to give Bones a hard stare. "But it is for you two."

Maddock focused on the chart while he spoke. "Has the group made a public announcement about finding Earhart's plane? I haven't heard anything in the news."

Bones gave him a mock scowl. "You wouldn't hear

about it unless they bought ad time on that public radio crap you listen to."

"Excuse me for not spending all my time reading about alien conspiracies," Maddock snapped.

The commander jumped in. "Actually, no public announcement has been made yet."

Maddock quickly recovered his composure. "So then how do you know they found it, or think they did?"

Roberts dropped his pencil and crossed his arms, his gaze becoming intense. "Without going beyond a need-to-know level of detail, SEALs, I can tell you that the Navy has a certain interest in Amelia Earhart's plane that has not been authorized for public disclosure at this time. Some time ago when the EARHART group announced within the commercial diving community that it was seeking divers to assist them with salvage efforts relating to Earhart's plane, the Navy responded to their request by posing as a commercial diving outfit. You two are going to work for them under that guise."

Bones held up a hand. "Excuse me, Sir. Wait just a minute, please. Do you mean to say that you're sending us on an undercover assignment?"

"That's exactly what I'm telling you, Bonebrake."

"Cool!" Bones sprang to his feet. "For some reason, I never get asked to go undercover. People think I stand out. No idea why." He lifted his chin and rose up a bit on the balls of his toes, emphasizing his height.

The commander did not smile.

Maddock gritted his teeth. Would Bones never stop? As his comrade settled back into his seat, Maddock returned his attention to the commander. "What are our specific objectives for this mission?"

Roberts nodded in his direction, probably grateful for Maddock's directing the briefing forward in a professional manner.

"What we need you to do is simple: If this group has actually located Earhart's plane, we need you to confirm that, and then we need you to recover certain assets from it if they can be found."

The commander paused to allow Maddock and Bones to absorb this.

"There are two major types of assets we're looking for that may be in or around the site of the plane wreck. "*One...*" Roberts said forcefully to regain their attention, "we're looking for any kind of photographic apparatus, especially undeveloped film, associated with Earhart's plane. Two: we need to recover anything resembling a porcelain or ceramic container, which—*pay attention* now—may still contain weaponized smallpox."

The commander leaned back in his chair as if ready to field an inevitable barrage of questions.

"Did you say *smallpox*?" Maddock clarified.

"I said *weaponized* smallpox, yes. Don't ask what she was doing with it, if it's even there. Your job is simply to find it and bring it back to us. If possible, keep even the EARHART team from knowing about its existence, but either way, get control of it and have it with you when you make the sat-phone call for extraction."

"Smallpox?" Bones repeated. "I don't think my people ever wrote a thank-you note to the white folks for that generous gift."

Maddock shuddered as he recalled images he'd seen of Native Americans suffering from the disease, their entire faces and bodies riddled with horrible-looking, pus-filled sores before they died.

Roberts managed a sympathetic look that lasted about a second. "In all likelihood the smallpox," he paused for a moment, seeking the right word, "...*containers* are no longer with the plane. Or if they are, they're most likely no longer intact after more than six decades of immersion in seawater following the plane crash."

"*Most likely?*" Bones made a sour face. "One time, this chick told me she 'most likely' didn't have herpes. Not too comforting."

The commander cleared his throat. "I agree."

He was about to continue when there came a knock at

the door. He told the person to come in, and a female Navy nurse in her late twenties wheeling a stainless steel medical cart entered the room.

"Set up right over there, please." The commander pointed to a corner of the room before quickly getting back to Maddock and Bones. He picked up a pair of manila folders. "That's why I've taken the liberty of accessing your medical histories." He opened one of the folders and leafed through its pages. "You two are..." He halted in mid-sentence. Maddock was following him Bones' gaze was on the nurse as she began unzipping some sort of kit. Roberts cleared his throat. "Bonebrake? You with us?"

Bones snapped his head back around. "Sorry, Commander."

"You two are too young to have gotten a smallpox vaccination as children. The U.S. stopped giving the vaccine in the early nineteen seventies after successful eradication efforts. We still stockpile it, though, just in case." He raised an eyebrow and tipped his head toward the nurse, who gave a welcoming smile as she held up a needle.

"Just in case of a weaponized attack against the U.S.?" Maddock asked.

"That's right. After all, because so many citizens have never been vaccinated against it, an outbreak would be catastrophic. It's quite contagious." Maddock nodded to acknowledge the response and then the commander said, "Please, walk over to Lieutenant Sanchez so that she can administer the vaccine to you. It's just a precaution."

Bones reached the nurse's station almost before Roberts finished his sentence, with Maddock walking up behind him.

"Okay, boys, roll up your sleeves. This won't hurt a bit." The nurse watched as Maddock and Bones presented their bare shoulders, and she quickly swabbed a portion of their skin with alcohol pads.

"This, on the other hand," she said, picking up a strange-looking bifurcated needle, "will most definitely hurt."

She dipped the two-pronged instrument into a flask and

jabbed it into Bones' shoulder, cutting off his laughter. He looked up at her in surprise.

"You're a tricky one!"

"You might be able to fool a couple of dolphins, but you're not getting past me."

Maddock presented his shoulder. "Heard about that, huh?"

"The whole ship heard about it." She picked up another of the needles and stuck it into Maddock's arm. She looked at him and frowned.

"Something wrong?

"No, it's just weird that you're a Navy guy and your eyes are the color of the sea. They're…" She paused, shook her head as if to clear her thoughts, and then resumed a professional air.

"It should turn red in a few hours, then in a day or so develop kind of an open sore. That's completely normal. Another day or so after that it'll scab over. If you experience a different progression than that, then notify a doctor when you get back." She glanced from Maddock to Bones and back to Maddock.

"Good luck, boys!" She began packing up her equipment.

Commander Roberts said, "Thank you, Lieutenant. Dismissed." He waited until she had wheeled her cart to the door and Bones held it open for her. When they were alone again, Roberts said, "In terms of what to expect on the dives, I'm told you'll be using traditional scuba air tanks for dives to a depth of two hundred ten feet, where the plane rests on a coral shelf."

"That's deep," Maddock said.

"We'll be deep undercover," Bones quipped, eliciting an eye roll from the commander, who continued.

"It is a demanding dive, which you'll be doing multiple times. Take care. The surface water is warm, but it's colder at two-hundred feet there than it is in the harbor here," he said, waving an arm at the water outside his office walls. "But there's more than that," he added before his two

SEALs could shrug. He knew they'd been through far worse conditions than that, and if anything would need to fake discomfort to match their fictitious backgrounds.

Both of them waited for him to speak. He looked down at his desk for a moment, almost as if uncomfortable. Then he said, "There have been reports of a strange sea creature or creatures in the area."

Maddock and Bones exchanged questioning glances. At length, Bones asked, "What kind of creatures?"

Roberts shrugged. "We're not sure. It might even be some kind of publicity stunt on the part of EARHART. Just stay alert down there at all times. That's all."

He stood and handed Maddock and Bones the briefing files. Maddock and Bones stood up to go.

"One more thing." They looked at their commander.

"In the chopper you'll find a backpack with a few supplies including a satellite phone and two digital cameras in waterproof housings. You will not be taking any firearms on this mission as it would be out of line with your cover story. Is that clear?"

"Yes sir," they both intoned.

Then, "Our dive gear?" Maddock wanted to know.

"All of it will be provided by the EARHART team. Don't bring your own, with the exception of minor accessories if you have a preference, and especially don't let on that you're used to using military equipment, understood?"

The two SEALs nodded, the nature of their undercover work now setting in.

"I can't deny I have reservations about sending the two of you on this mission." The commander's voice sharpened as he spoke. "You come highly recommended, but you also have the reputation of being a couple of buffoons. Nothing I've seen in this meeting has dissuaded me that the latter is true, at least when it comes to one of you." He turned a flinty gaze upon Bones.

"We won't let you down," Bones said, suddenly chastened.

"I hope not. Good luck, gentlemen. I look forward to debriefing you after a successful mission."

After saluting their superior officer, Maddock and Bones walked to the door.

"Smallpox," Bones muttered as he looked at his shoulder while they exited the room. "Why'd it have to be smallpox?"

When they stepped out of the office the sailor who had escorted them here was waiting outside the door. "This way, please."

He smiled at them and waved toward the expansive stern deck, where a helicopter's rotors began to turn.

CHAPTER 3

Orona Atoll, Phoenix Islands, Republic of Kiribati

"That's our island." The pilot of the Sikorsky pointed down at a ring of coral set against a dazzling blue backdrop. A non-military charter pilot who knew nothing about his passengers other than they were part of an expedition to find Amelia Earhart's plane, he engaged in some radio chatter as he banked the craft toward the designated landing spot.

In the rear passenger seat, Maddock and Bones gazed down at their destination. They were travel-weary after nearly fifteen hours in the air; Honolulu was already a distant memory to them, like a dream. Manila was a blur of airport red tape that ended with them boarding the chopper over an hour ago.

"*That's* it?" Bones squinted out the window. "I thought that was just a cloud shadow."

"That's probably what Amelia Earhart thought, too. We're at the same altitude, one thousand feet, that she was coming in at looking for Howland."

"You bring a lot of people out here?" Maddock held his new digital camera up to the window and took an aerial snapshot of the island. He knew from experience that it might come in handy. The atoll consisted of a thin strip of land in a rough oval shape surrounding a shallow, turquoise-colored lagoon. The outer edges of the land featured sandy beaches, while the middle of the ribbon-like land mass was green with scrub forest and coconut palms.

"I've been to the Phoenix chain before, but this is my fist time to Orona. Pretty much nobody goes here, ever. Hold on," the pilot finished, indicating that he needed to focus on the landing. Maddock and Bones gripped the hand straps hanging from the ceiling as the pilot brought the aircraft lower until the tops of the palm trees bent with the force of their rotor wash.

As they leveled out and skirted the treetops, Maddock looked out along the atoll and spotted the tallest man-made structure on the island—a radio antenna atop a metal tower. A few tent-like structures were set up at the base of it. Bones pointed over to one end of the island where a seaplane and a small boat floated beside a modest pier. In a clearing on one of the larger strips of land where it flared out before continuing on as a thin ribbon, an encampment was visible as a rag-tag patchwork of multi-colored tents. That was all there was on the atoll. Everything else was just sand, coral, jungle, lagoon and ocean.

Far out to sea Maddock spotted what must have been a sizable ship to be visible at this distance. Other than that, the ocean, too, seemed empty.

Did it conceal Amelia Earhart's airplane?

Maddock didn't have long to wonder because they soon were dropping down vertically into a cleared area not far from the camp. On the ground, a group of three men waited, shielding their faces from the blowing coral dust kicked up by the chopper's rotors. One of them was taking pictures of the chopper as it landed.

The pilot turned around to face them. "This is where you get off. I've got to get back to Manila. Enjoy your stay and good luck!"

Maddock and Bones grabbed their backpacks and jumped from the helicopter onto the coral island. Immediately they felt the sunlight on their backs and the humidity in their lungs. They ducked until clear of the rotors. When they stood straight again a man of average build somewhere in his sixties was standing in front of them, hand extended. He wore a khaki outfit complete with wide-brimmed straw hat, sunglasses and leather flip-flops. He sported a bushy white beard and mustache. Two other men stood beside him, one of them snapping pictures of Maddock and Bones with a 35mm camera. EARHART already had their photos as part of their bogus employee files from the "dive company," but still, it wasn't comforting to know they were being photographed while actually on a mission.

"Welcome to the Phoenix Islands," the man with the beard said, pumping Maddock's hand and then Bones' rapidly in turn. There was no real enthusiasm to the greeting. He was just going through the motions. "First time?"

"That's right," Maddock said. Bones nodded in agreement.

"Hopefully we find this damn plane and you have a trip to remember. Something to tell the grandkids, right?" Grandkids were the furthest possible thing from Bones' mind, but he smiled and laughed politely.

"I'm Fred Spinney, Director of The EARHART Group and leader of this expedition."

Maddock steeled himself for a convincing delivery. "Jim Abott, sir, from Deep Star Divers. Nice to meet you."

Spinney nodded and then looked at Bones, who said, "Keith Winslow, also from Deep Star. Great to meet you."

"Wow, I thought your name might be Running Bear or something like that!" Spinney looked at one of the men standing next to him as if to see how big a laugh he had elicited, but the short, pudgy man with a sweaty forehead only shook his head and extended a hand.

"That's funny," Bones said to Spinney. "Actually, they call me Crapper because I chew annoying white guys up and… well, you get the picture."

Spinney's jaw dropped and Bones smiled and winked. "Just messing with you guys. I'll answer to Winslow or Keith, either one."

Maddock gave Bones' foot a subtle kick. *Don't rile this guy up too much.*

"Pleased to make your acquaintance, gentlemen. I'm Steve Carlson, Director of Research for The EARHART Group." He dutifully pumped Maddock and Bones' hands.

"Steve, here, is a big part of the reason we knew to look on this island, to find Earhart's plane out of all the places it could be," Spinney said.

Maddock and Bones nodded politely and the other man with Spinney stepped forward. "G'day. I'm George Taylor, expedition topside photographer. I shoot pictures and video of everything that doesn't take place underwater." He spoke in an Australian accent and had piercing blue eyes. He wore tattered shorts and flip-flops as well as a beige photographer's vest festooned with photographic paraphernalia.

As soon as Maddock and Bones finished shaking Taylor's hand, Spinney said, "Brace yourselves."

The helicopter lifted off and the men turned away from the blowing dust until the craft was well overhead. They watched it turn and then head off in a northwesterly direction until it was a mere yellow speck in the sky, the sound of birds chattering once again the loudest noise on the atoll.

"That's probably the most traffic we'll see here until our next supply drop in two weeks," Spinney stated. "If there's one thing this place has in spades, it's peace and quiet. But we're early to bed, early to rise, here, so it works out for the best."

He pointed down a sandy track that led away from the landing area. "Let's get on over to camp, shall we?"

Spinney, Carlson and Taylor led the way, with Maddock and Bones ambling close behind. As they walked, Spinney peppered them with questions without looking back.

"So you came out from California, is that it? Long flight, how was it?"

Maddock and Bones said they thought it wasn't bad.

"Good, so you feel up to getting right to work?"

Truthfully, after being whisked halfway around the world following their training exercise and having only aircraft to sleep on and eat from for the past two days, they were ready for a sleeping bag. But they were SEALs, and SEALs could go and go and go if they had to, plus they had a mission objective to achieve and so getting right to work appealed to them. Still, although a couple of divers new on the job might want to appear eager to please their employer, they didn't want to appear *over* eager, lest it would somehow tip Spinney off to their cover.

So Maddock said, "Sure, we'll get settled into camp, meet the dive team, get briefed on the site, right? Dive first thing tomorrow?"

Spinney bellowed a hearty guffaw that caused a small flock of birds to take to the air from where they'd been roosting in a bush. "How about we do all of those things, *and* you make your first dive today to get acquainted with the wreck site? Nothing strenuous. Just get down there, have a look-see. You up for that?"

While this was actually preferable for Maddock and Bones, Maddock couldn't help but think that a civilian employee would feel coerced into making the dive whether he wanted to or not. It could potentially be a safety issue, and was the first tiny red flag for Maddock that Spinney was willing to play fast and loose with the safety of others in order to meet his goal of finding and ultimately raising that plane.

"Dive today? Sure, whatever you think is best."

"No problem," Bones added.

"That's what I like to hear!" Spinney followed the path as it traced the curving beach of the island and then pointed ahead. "Camp's up this way."

They emerged through a patch of foliage into a grassy clearing.

"This is the highest point on the island." Spinney took an exaggerated couple of steps up a small rise as if to underscore this point. "Elevation three feet!"

A small tent city stood in the clearing, which was ringed on three sides by vegetation and the beach on the fourth.

"C'mon, I'll give you the grand tour." Spinney led them to the radio tower they saw from the helicopter, situated on the edge of camp. An open tent at the base of it held folding tables stacked with electronic equipment. Portable solar panels ringed the communications tent.

Spinney pointed to the lone man inside the tent, who, because he was wearing headphones, could not hear them.

"This is our Communications Director, Harvey Sims. Pretty much the only reliable means of communication with the rest of the world from out here is via shortwave radio, so Harvey keeps us in touch."

Sims sat in a folding chair in front of the gear. Spinney walked into the tent and tapped him on the shoulder. The man jumped in his chair, apparently spooked. Upon seeing it was Spinney, with others behind him, the man smiled sheepishly and stood.

Like Spinney, this man also sported a full beard, but his was black. His jocular cheeks were pale, with a tinge of sunburn to them.

"Sorry, Harvey, didn't mean to startle you. Maybe ease up on the coffee?"

Sims waved at his radio gear. "I was tuned into your chopper's air band," he said, looking at Maddock and Bones. "Your pilot just told the tower in Manila he was glad to drop you two bozos off!" This elicited peals of laughter from Spinney.

Maddock and Bones smiled good-naturedly.

Sims appeased them. "Kidding. I was tracking a faint signal from Germany, straining to hear through some solar flare interference when you tapped me. So these are the new kids on the block?"

Spinney nodded and introduced Maddock and Bones, who cordially greeted the radio operator under their assumed identities.

"In any kind of emergency," Spinney explained, "Harvey, here, is our lifeline. He can reach just about anywhere to get a message out."

Carlson addressed Maddock and Bones. "A lot of amateur radio operators around the Pacific Rim reported receiving signals from Amelia Earhart in the hours *after* her plane was calculated to have run out of fuel, indicating that she had either landed somewhere or perhaps her plane floated for a while before it sank."

"Sank right here on this atoll!" Spinney added with relish.

"We're here to help confirm that for you." Maddock felt weird looking Spinney in the eye while uttering such a half-truth, but technically it was correct. Bones gave a big grin while nodding, but he said nothing.

"Speaking of, let's get to it." Spinney stepped away from the radio station.

"Good luck and dive safe!" Sims told them before turning back to his equipment.

Maddock and Bones once again fell in behind Spinney, Carlson and Taylor. Maddock spoke softly as they walked away from the radio shack.

"Seems like an awful lot of people are wishing us luck lately."

"You noticed it, too?

They walked across the cleared area, passing two Pacific Islanders who were washing dishes under a lean-to. Spinney waved to them but did not offer introductions. On the other side of the clearing they reached a large tarp suspended from a group of palms, under which was a gas generator powering an air compressor. One man, clad only in a wetsuit from the waist down, monitored the compressor's gauges, while another in identical dress was loading scuba tanks into a wheelbarrow. Two more men were rinsing additional scuba equipment in buckets of fresh water.

Spinney raised his voice over the compressor's hum and rattle. "Gentlemen, please meet the newest members of our dive team—your new colleagues." At this all four men under the tarp looked over at Maddock and Bones with interest. Names were given, including the cover names Maddock and Bones were getting used to using.

"So, you think you can work together?" Spinney demanded of his lead diver. The man nodded, looking at the two new divers. "Checked out your resumes. Impressive. Did some North Sea oil rig work myself, back in the day, We'll have to compare war stories."

Maddock and Bones had in fact dove on an oil rig in the North Sea, but it was in support of a clandestine Naval operation, not a commercial job. But they played the part, nodding and smiling, Bones saying how he'd buy the drinks if they ever got off this piece of coral.

Spinney looked at his watch before addressing his diver. "Good. So you're the only one not requiring a surface interval, right?"

The man nodded. Maddock and Bones knew he was referring to time off between dives to avoid the bends, caused by a buildup of nitrogen in the bloodstream.

Spinney continued. "Then get a move on. Whichever one of you can do the longest dive now according to your computers, take these two down to the site. You don't have to do the whole dive with them, just bring them down to the plane. They can make the rest of the first dive themselves, am I right?" He stared critically at Maddock and Bones, who merely nodded, thinking how perfect it was to be left alone on the site.

"Oh, almost forgot." Spinney picked up a folder that lay on a nearby table and pulled some photos out of it. "Here are first images of the plane. Like we said, it's stuck under a coral shelf on the edge of the reef in more than two-hundred feet of water."

He handed Maddock and Bones the printouts while the divers looked on. Maddock and Bones studied the grainy shots of a sunken, historic airplane.

Spinney looked over their shoulders at the photo. "Looks like an Electra model 10-E to me! But let's get you down for a closer look. We still need a serial number to confirm it."

Spinney clapped his hands in a chop-chop fashion as he looked at his dive team. "Get 'er done. I want these new guys up to speed quick-like."

Then he, Carlson and Taylor, who was hastily taking snapshots of the divers talking to Maddock and Bones, departed the dive tent.

"You heard the man." The diver who'd given his name only as 'Bugsy' tossed a couple of wetsuits at Maddock and Bones.

"Let's do this!"

CHAPTER 4

An hour later, Maddock, Bones and Bugsy stepped aboard an inflatable Zodiac boat tied to one side of the small pier Maddock had seen from the helicopter. A blue seaplane was tied to the other side of the pier. A squat, muscular Asian American man greeted them from behind the boat's steering console.

"Bruce Watanabe, pleased to meet you."

"Likewise," Maddock shook his hand. Undercover or not, the boat operator was the guy who would be driving them to and from the dive site, and they wanted to be on good terms with him if at all possible.

"It's not the Love Boat but it'll do, right?" Bones offered his infectious grin, which Watanabe returned.

"Hey, if we confirm this plane is actually Earhart's, we all plan to have a celebration at one of the resort islands—drinks on Spinney!"

"Sounds good to me," Bones returned. And it did. But he felt a pang of regret since he knew those drinks would never come, at least not with anyone from Spinney's team. His job was to get those assets off the plane and return them to the U.S. Navy. Only then would he be celebrating.

"That the break in the reef, there?" Maddock pointed to a notch in the atoll brimming with whitewater. Like Bones, he too was thinking forward to the mission and getting it done.

Watanabe nodded and Bugsy responded.

"Water in the lagoon has been calm for us in the morning with a light wind kicking up by afternoon. There's a passage in the atoll through the surf line. Once we get through that the dive site's usually not too choppy. But the currents underwater are wicked. Let's get out there and I'll brief you some more when we're on site."

Watanabe put the boat into gear and they raced across

the calm lagoon at a good clip. The water here was shallow and gin-clear. To Maddock it looked as though they were about to hit various coral formations growing on the bottom. Watanabe and Bugsy were obviously used to it, not appearing concerned in the least. Maddock and Bones enjoyed the feel of the salt spray on their faces as the boat glided across the lagoon.

In a couple of minutes Watanabe eased back on the throttle and the Zodiac slowed as it approached a cut in the coral ring. Fast-moving water sloshed around in the opening, waves splashing against its sides.

"Hold on!" Watanabe gunned the outboard and they rocketed through the channel into open ocean. A couple of minutes later they approached an orange marker buoy.

"Wreck's a little ways out there," Bugsy said, pulling on his wetsuit, "but we'll follow the buoy line down to the shallow reef and get situated. From there we'll swim out to the edge of the drop-off and head down to the wreck."

"Sounds good." Maddock and Bones pulled their gear on.

"So like we discussed, as soon as we come within sight of the airplane, I'm going to head back to the boat. I've done too many deep dives lately and I've got to go again tomorrow. But you two will stay down there to check out the site."

Maddock and Bones completed a check of each others' gear and said they were ready.

"So you've used the full facemasks with comm gear before, right?"

The masks Maddock and Bones wore were not standard dive masks, and not helmets either, but something in between. They were rubber and covered the entire face, but not the whole head. This meant that the divers could breathe through their noses, and talk through integrated transmitters, while underwater. Bugsy moved to a box lying on the deck containing some electronic gear. He keyed a transmitter while looking at Maddock and Bones.

"You hear me in there?"

"Get out of my freaking head, man!" Bones joked. Both he and Maddock were intimately familiar with underwater communications gear, but he played the part of someone for whom it was still somewhat of a novelty.

"I hear you loud and clear." Maddock's voice was audible not only to Bugsy and the boat driver, but also to Bones.

"Great, so we'll be able to talk during our dive, and Bruce will be able to hear us up here. Ready?"

Maddock and Bones moved to one side of the boat while Bugsy went to the other. The three of them flopped backward into the water. As soon as the bubbles from their splashes cleared, they could see the bottom of the ocean thirty feet below as though they stood in the shallow end of a swimming pool.

"Nice clear water," Maddock said, testing the comm channel.

"Like a Jacuzzi, too, only with you two clowns instead of a couple of babes and some champagne," Bones said. After San Diego, the tropical ocean felt like a warm bath.

Bugsy's voice came over the frequency. "Yeah, up here we're practically burning up, but believe me, two hundred feet down you'll be glad for the suits. Bruce, you hear us?"

"Copy that, I hear all three of you."

Bugsy nodded at Maddock and Bones as he wrapped a hand around the buoy line. "Down we go. And we may not have champagne, but if you're not careful the nitrogen narcosis will give you a nice buzz." In addition to the bends, another danger of deep diving was the narcotic effect nitrogen could have on the brain; like having a few beers in a short amount of time, it affected judgment. Bugsy jerked a thumb downwards and the trio vented the air from their buoyancy compensator vests and began to sink.

They reached the bottom and Bugsy pointed down the slope. "This way." The flat sandy bottom studded with patches of coral now gave way to a steep incline covered in a riot of hard corals and sea fans, like an underwater garden. Small, colorful fish darted about, and exotic-looking shrimp and crabs scuttled between coral formations. Maddock looked up one last time before the slope transitioned to a near-vertical incline and saw the silhouette of their boat limned against the tropical sun.

"Now we drop down the wall." Bugsy led them over the edge. Maddock felt the pressure increasing in his ears. His full-face mask making it impossible to "equalized" them with the so-called Valsalva Maneuver, pinching his nose closed and blowing into it, he made do by flexing his jaw muscles while thrusting the jawbone forward. It was less effective than the Valsalva, but the best he could do. He felt his ears pop and instantly the pain stopped.

"Nice jaw work," Bones said. "My grandmother had a bulldog that used to make the exact same face."

"No, that was my barracuda imitation," Dane said, and then laughed when Bones, clearly feeling the pressure, worked his own jaw in the same fashion. They'd have to do it every few seconds from here on out.

"You guys know a bit about diving, I see." Bugsy sounded impressed.

The light grew dimmer as they descended. When they reached a depth of one hundred feet, a large form startled them by swimming out from a crevice just beneath them.

"Grouper." Bugsy pointed to the large fish as it swam off.

"Gotta be the size of my old VW bus." Maddock shot Bones a warning look. He really did used to have a VW bus, which Maddock knew from all of the sordid tales he'd regaled his fellow SEALs with. They were under cover and divulging any details about their true identities was a risk. Bones gave him a subtle nod to indicate he understood. "Deep undercover" may have seemed like a joke back in the commander's office, but now it was as real as ever.

They descended in silence until, at a depth of 185 feet they reached a large coral overhang. At this depth the growth was more stunted, due to the low ambient sunlight.

"Lights on." Bugsy flipped on his powerful halogen dive light and Maddock and Bones did the same. They swept their beams around the uneven shelf. Bugsy stood and walked backward, waving as he dropped over its edge. "Down we go again!"

Maddock and Bones swam over the ledge, shining their light beams down, watching Bugsy sink into a black void. Once beneath the overhang, Maddock swept his beam toward the wall and saw that an opening extended many yards back.

Partially blocking this opening was an airplane.

Parts of it still appeared silver in color, but most of it was encrusted with dark-colored marine growth. Maddock shone his beam along the fuselage toward the nose of the plane, which extended into a tunnel in the coral wall. He judged the plane to be about forty feet in length, which, according to the briefing material he'd read on the flight over, was about right for the Lockheed Electra the aviatrix was flying when she vanished.

"Okay, boys. This is it. It's definitely an Electra, but we have yet to confirm that it's Earhart's with a serial number. We already looked under the wings where the numbers are painted but they're totally encrusted over with barnacles and crap. But there's a brass number plate up in the cockpit that should have held up well enough that we can clean it up enough to read it. Thing is, as you can see, the cockpit is way up into a depression in the rock, there, almost as if there was a collapse of the wall around the plane at some point, possibly during an earthquake."

They heard the rasp of Bugsy's breathing as he sucked in the dense air at this depth.

"We'll check it out." Maddock motioned for Bones to scout the right side of the plane while he took the left. Before long Maddock could hear Bones' labored breathing as he rounded the plane's nose.

"Kicking almost as hard as I can to get around this thing," Bones' voice came over the comm unit.

"Roger that," Bugsy said. "It's something you're going to need to get used to. I'm headed back topside. Watch your air gauges, guys, you don't have a lot of time down here, especially fighting that current." The deeper a diver went and the more he exerted himself, the less time his air supply lasted. This dive was very deep, almost at the limit of where scuba divers using air could go.

Maddock acknowledged the response. "Copy that. See you topside in a few."

Bugsy waved as he swam toward the distant sunlight, leaving Maddock and Bones alone with the plane wreck.

Was it Earhart's?

"You've got to see this," Bones said from the other side of the plane. Maddock continued his path a bit farther before confirming that the cockpit was indeed not accessible from this side.

"Copy that, coming around." He also stopped at the rear cargo door but it was encrusted shut. When they had left for the boat they'd been warned by Steve Carlson, the researcher, not to cause any damage to the plane, by prying at it with a dive knife, for example.

"See what?" Bugsy's voice reminded them that they were not on a private channel.

"Bullet holes. Looks like this thing was strafed by machine gun fire. I don't think Amelia Earhart was a dogfighter, was she?"

Maddock paused to hold his dive knife, which had ruler markings etched onto the blade, and held it across one of the holes. "Looks like it to me." Privately, he thought the holes consistent with 50-caliber slugs, but he didn't want to raise suspicion by appearing too knowledgeable. He then made his way around the plane's tail section toward Bones.

"Let's not rule anything out." This from Bugsy, swimming somewhere above. "Until we have that serial number, we won't take anything for granted."

Normally Maddock would agree that evidence of aerial warfare made it unlikely to be the plane Earhart was flying. But when combined with being asked to look for weaponized smallpox in conjunction with her aircraft? He wasn't so sure. There was one thing he was certain of, though, and that was that he had to keep these thoughts from Bugsy, so he said nothing of the sort over the comm line.

Maddock swam over to Bones, who was brushing a gloved hand over the bullet holes in the plane's fuselage. Maddock swam past him toward the nose of the plane on the right side. He couldn't see any way to penetrate inside it yet. This far back beneath the ledge it was very dark, and he depended almost exclusively on his dive light to be able to see any detail. A few fish swam by him but there was not nearly as much life down here as up on the shallow reef. He swept his light beam around the airplane's cockpit, the doors wedged in between two walls of a narrow cave-like space. No way in without damaging the plane. He was hoping to be able to reach the cockpit windows, which were likely broken, but they were farther up into the tight space.

"Jim, what's your pressure gauge read, buddy? I'm getting low, myself."

Maddock was looking up and to the right of the plane, where there was a tunnel-like opening near the back of the overhang's ceiling.

"*Jim*, you copy?"

Maddock knew that Bones would think he wasn't recognizing his cover name. He was already feeling a little tipsy from the heavy nitrogen loads at this depth. But that wasn't it. He scanned his light beam at the opening near the ceiling. *Looks like a tunnel that might lead somewhere...*

"*Jim!*"

"Sorry, Keith, I copy." He started to tell Bones how he had found what might be a passage through the coral back into where the plane's cockpit was, but checked the impulse. Bugsy and Bruce were listening.

"Copy that. Read your pressure gauge."

Maddock checked his air gauge. "One thousand psi. Time to go." Exploring the opening would have to wait.

"Copy. Meet me at the tail and we'll head up together."

"On my way."

Bones was waiting in front of the Electra's tail section when Maddock got there. Both of them were breathing hard to avoid being swept off the ledge into the open void.

Maddock gave Bones the thumbs-up signal, signifying he was ready to ascend. The two of them pushed off the ledge toward the light, over two-hundred feet above. As soon as they did, Maddock felt something brush against his wetsuit. He turned to the left, away from the wall, in time to see a large, sleek torpedo shape shoot past them, arcing out into open water.

"What was that?"

"Did you see that?" Maddock and Bones spoke at the same time, over one another. Maddock saw a glint of metal in his light as Bones freed his dive knife from the sheath on his calf, but they saw no sign of whatever it was that had rushed past them.

"See what?" This from Bugsy.

"Not sure." Maddock kept moving up, with Bones right beside him. Low on air with large creatures in the vicinity was no time to hang around at two-hundred feet.

"We're heading back to the reef now."

They reached the shallow, flat reef without further incident and there they performed a decompression stop, simply breathing their air at a shallow depth for several minutes, to avoid the bends. That completed, they ascended the buoy line and surfaced next to the waiting boat.

CHAPTER 5

Maddock, Bones and the entire EARHART Group team were gathered around a campfire. Dinner had been finished and now the group relaxed, some enjoying a dessert of tangy, exotic fruits while others sipped on cold South Pacific Lager from a cooler. The meal itself, fresh-caught reef fish and rice, had been eaten largely in silence, the team hungry and tired after a day's work outdoors and underwater. Maddock and Bones were particularly exhausted, and they knew that tomorrow they faced a long, full day of undercover, underwater work. Yet getting to know the team was important, and they had questions they wanted answered.

Some of these focused on tomorrow's dives, and logistics were discussed at length. They were glad to hear that they'd be doing the first dive of the day alone. Maddock and Bones made subtle eye contact that said, *that's our chance.* Neither had yet mentioned anything about the possible tunnel Maddock had found. As he stared into the crackling flames, Maddock wondered if it would help them access the plane. And if it did, that brought up a question that was on all the team's minds, although it was Bones who voiced it for everyone.

"If that is Amelia's plane, then there's a good chance that her and her navigator's bodies are still in there, right?"

Many in the group nodded. Steve Carlson responded. "It is likely, although all that would be left by now would be a couple of skeletons. Those, of course, would have to be DNA tested for additional confirmation."

The group contemplated this in silence for a few moments until Maddock looked across the fire at Spinney and asked, "If it does turn out to be her plane, do you intend to raise it, or is finding it and retrieving artifacts from it as far as you plan to go?"

"This particular expedition is only to confirm whether the plane we found is Earhart's and to recover easily accessible artifacts, but if that goes well a full-scale salvage operation would be on the table for a future expedition."

"Hopefully we can be a part of it." Bones took a swig of his beer.

"Do a good job on this trip and it could happen," Spinney said. After a slight pause, he added, "Bugsy tells me you two did well down there today. Saw the wreck. What do you think? You up for a couple weeks' worth of diving down there?"

Maddock and Bones nodded enthusiastically. "There is one thing that gave us some concern today," Maddock said. He told them about the sleek animal that brushed past them on the ledge.

"What do you think that was, a shark?" Bones asked.

They were met with a surprisingly uncomfortable silence.

"Sorry, did I say something wrong? Somebody get bit once?"

Spinney shook his head and held up a hand as if to ward off any other replies. "I'm sorry you had to see that. We were hoping that threat has passed. It's been a few days since we've seen it, but it seems our friends at Mizuhi Development Corporation are at it again."

Bones looked confused. "Mizuhi Development?"

"Yes, it's a Japanese consortium of land development companies. They've had some designs on this little atoll. They put in some offers to buy it from the Kiribati Republic in the last few years, all of which were rejected. But as soon as we announced we may have found Earhart's plane here, that's when they really ramped up their efforts to buy the island." Spinney's visage took on a darker mood.

"What do they want to do with it?" Bones asked, looking out at the edge of the campsite into the dark wilderness.

Spinney sipped from a coffee mug featuring the words, "Today's the day!" and set it down on a rock. "Build a luxury tourist resort. I've seen the conceptual renderings. Overwater bungalows, fine dining, winding paths lit by tiki torches, the whole nine yards."

"Hey, we've practically got all that already!" One of the divers joked.

Spinney smiled and went on. "They'll clear the main jungle and put lodge-style buildings there. The whole beach will have piers and bungalows. Paved helipad and airstrip over there. Big concrete docking pier for large yachts, possibly even cruise ships." He pointed away from the camp. "But the clincher would be the plane. There's no shortage of luxury resorts to choose from in this part of the world. But imagine if this one had Amelia Earhart's airplane hanging from the ceiling of the main lodge, over the bar, and they call the place, 'The Lost Explorer Resort' or some crap like that."

"I'd have a few rounds at that bar," Bones admitted. Maddock shook his head while Spinney frowned in his direction.

"Yeah, well a lot of people would, I expect. I'm sure their market research told them as much. Even if this plane turns out not to be Earhart's, which I doubt, I think they'd still try to market it that way. So that's why they've been trying to scare us off lately."

Maddock looked Spinney in the eye. "Scare you off how?"

All eyes were on Spinney. Maddock suspected it wasn't because no one else knew the answer to the question, but because they didn't want to answer it without Spinney's permission. The cacophony of nighttime insects and small, unseen animals pervaded the air.

"The creature you saw—do you think it could have been a small whale?"

Maddock and Bones traded glances. Maddock answered. "Could have, yes. We didn't get a good look, though. It brushed against my wetsuit, so I couldn't actually feel it, either."

"It was the whale," one of the divers said.

Bones looked perplexed. "*The* whale? There's only one out here?"

Spinney fielded the question. "There's only one that's been trained to attack our divers whenever they get near the plane wreck."

Spinney's revelation was met with uncharacteristic silence from Bones. Maddock frowned and considered the possibility that their military handlers had known about this threat. As coincidences went, an exercise against trained ocean-going mammals followed by a live encounter with one on the very next mission, would be a big one

No one was saying anything, so Maddock ventured, "You say, 'trained' whale?"

"Like Free Willy!" Bones exclaimed. To Maddock's relief, Bones didn't make his usual genitalia joke that accompanied the name of the movie whale.

Spinney shook his head. "Definitely not like Willy. First of all, it's not an Orca, but a pilot whale."

"Pilot whale?" Maddock said, feigning ignorance. He knew from his training that the small whale had been used in the past as a candidate for the U.S. Navy marine mammal program, before dolphins and sea lions became the go-to species.

"Yeah, it's technically a large dolphin, related to the killer whale. We think Mizuhi has been keeping one on their ship, training it to swim little sorties against us."

One of the divers raised a hand. "Last week the thing rammed me in the ribs something fierce on my way back up the wall."

"And it's been getting more aggressive lately," another diver chimed in. "But until today it had been about a week since any of us had seen it, so we thought maybe they gave up, or they lost it or something. At least, we hoped."

"Lost it?" Maddock prodded.

"Yeah, like it just decided the free meals weren't all that great compared to what it can catch in the wild and so it didn't return to the ship one day," Spinney said.

"That reminds me..." Maddock looked around the

group, who were watching him intently. "Flying in on the helicopter I did see a ship out there—a large, white one, miles out."

"That's Mizuhi's ship," Spinney confirmed with a nod. "So they are still around." "Off to greener pastures, or bluer waters, or whatever."

Harvey Sims pulled some errant pieces of fish from his beard and said, "I have heard an increase in Japanese chatter on the marine VHF bands lately, although I have no idea what they're saying. But I'll keep a close watch on it."

Spinney nodded his approval, and then turned back to Maddock and Bones. "Anyway, Mizuhi Corp is trying to drive us away. At first they tried legally, in the courts, which is nothing new if you're an undersea treasure hunter or salvor of artifacts. Happens all the time. Only difference is, when they lost their case in Kiribati's highest court, based on some tenuous claim to this island, instead of that being the end of it, they turned to intimidation. Initially, there were verbal confrontations, minor altercations where they would basically harass us by telling us to go home. But of course we told them to piss off."

Steve Carlson continued. "And not long after that is when the pilot whale started showing up on the wreck site."

Bones grimaced and clenched his fists, clearly having trouble containing his anger. A small whale trained to kill people was no minor danger. "Thanks for letting us know about that threat ahead of time," he directed at Spinney. Maddock reached around and knuckled him in the back. If Spinney got mad enough to fire them, they wouldn't be able to complete their mission.

Spinney threw up his hands. "I told you, I thought that threat had passed. Before today it was about a week since we'd last seen it. Am I right?" He swiveled his head around at his team, seeking corroboration.

They nodded and murmured monosyllabic grunts of affirmation, but it was clear that Bones' statement had resonated with them. It was part of the reason the group had sought additional divers, after all.

"No worries," Maddock said, seeking to placate Spinney. "We're aware of this whale now, and tomorrow we'll know to watch out for it. Right, Keith?" He gave Bones a hard stare.

"You bet. It's just a *small* whale trained to kill us, anyway. Not a big one."

The group laughed and Spinney gave a half-smile before glancing at his dive watch. "And on that note, I'm calling it a night, gentlemen. I suggest you do the same. Long day tomorrow."

CHAPTER 6

The next morning, soon after sunrise, Maddock and Bones rode in the Zodiac with Bruce Watanabe, this time his only passengers. The two SEALs each sat on one of the inflatable boat's pontoons, riding out to the marker buoy in silence. They would have the first dive of the day on the plane to themselves. They knew this would be a huge opportunity to further their mission agenda before they were working in close contact with Spinney's men.

Once anchored on the site Maddock and Bones strapped their gear on and splashed into the water. "Comm check, you hear me?" Watanabe's voice in their facemask headsets was a reminder that although they were alone, what they said to each other was being monitored.

Maddock responded, "Loud and clear," and then he and Bones dropped down along the buoy line. They followed the same path they'd swum with Bugsy and within a few minutes were staring once again at the sunken plane.

Maddock spoke inside his face mask. "Topside, we are on the plane, going to have a look around, over."

Watanabe's reply was instant. "Copy that."

Maddock and Bones had already discussed their plans for the dive in secret last night after the campfire, and the two of them headed straight for the opening Maddock had seen in the ledge. The water was clear and it was easy to see where they were going. They flicked their dive lights on, rounded the plane's tail and swam under the wing. Maddock pointed up into the opening in the ceiling. Bones nodded.

"Topside, we've located a possible opening in the coral wall. We're going to see if it might lead anywhere."

Watanabe's voice came back immediately. "Topside here: copy that. Be advised that we may lose communication if you get deep into a tunnel, over."

"Copy."

Maddock finned upward to the ceiling of the cavern where the cockpit of the plane disappeared into the coral wall. Bones was right behind him. They swam up over the lip of the entrance and into an irregular chamber. They were greeted with a solid wall only a few feet in front of them, but rough passages led off to the right and left. Colorful sponges and tubeworms covered the walls and ceiling. Maddock played his light around the confined area for a few seconds before pointing left.

"Plane's that way, so let's check this tunnel first."

"Right behind you."

Although it was fairly high—a tall man could stand inside with headroom to spare—the tunnel wasn't wide enough for both divers to swim side-by-side. Maddock moved slowly into the passage, shining his light in a slow arc as he went. Ahead the tunnel curved to the left and they followed it, only to have it jog back right. It also became a little lower and more narrow.

"Good thing I'm not claustrophobic, Bones said. "Right about now I wish I was your puny size. If this thing gets any smaller I'm gonna be like a cork in a bottle."

It was a thought that gave him pause. One negative about diving this deep and in a confined space without the rest of the team meant that if anything went wrong they were on their own. Sure, Watanabe would know what happened, but it wouldn't do them any good. By the time anyone from the team got all the way down here, they'd have run out of air.

"Up here it forks," Maddock said. "The passage we're in leads down while another one goes off to the right. Let's take the low road."

"I usually do. Low road, copy that."

Maddock continued along the tunnel down until it flared out and ended abruptly—opening into a large space below.

"Dropping into a room...." Maddock wanted Bones to have a heads up. They could not afford to get separated. Another thing he found alarming was that without their lights it would be pitch black in the tunnels. Besides their main flashlights, they each carried a small backup light clipped to their vests, but still, being lost in a pitch black maze two-hundred feet underwater wasn't something he liked to contemplate.

Maddock allowed himself to drift to the floor of the cave. He stood there with his fins flat on the bottom. A medium-sized fish gave him a <u>start</u> as it came face-to-mask with him and then darted off. As soon as he saw Bones' light beam sweep the chamber, he took off again, swimming slowly and cautiously around a large coral protuberance.

There, occupying almost the entire enclosed space, was the cockpit of the old airplane. Maddock stared up at it in wonder. When they were first told they were looking for Amelia Earhart's airplane he'd pictured a small craft, perhaps a rickety old wooden plane befitting the 1930s. However, from the briefing he learned it was, of course, metal—a Lockheed Electra. And he'd been given the approximate dimensions, too, but seeing it down here right in front of him gave him a whole new perspective. It was a *big* aircraft, towering above him. In his mind's eye he envisioned skinny Amelia climbing up into the cockpit from the ladder steps, giving a last wave to the crowd gathered on the runway.

The main body of the plane was on the other side of the coral wall. He could see now that much of the wall above had crumbled and broken in on the craft, trapping it here. It would not be easy to extricate, if possible at all.

But that was Spinney's problem. He and Bones just need to see what was in it and get it out. Presently the large Indian swam up beside him, illuminating the aircraft.

"Nice! You see that?"

He held his beam in one place—the cockpit window.

Maddock nodded. "All the glass has been busted out." They watched as a fish swam out through the broken windscreen.

He consulted his pressure gauge. This was not the place to run out of air.

"Let's hurry up and get it done."

Maddock pressed the button on his BCD to add air to his vest, creating a soft *pfft*, and then he pushed gently off the bottom, rising to the level of the windscreen.

"Looks like it popped out completely." Maddock positioned himself to swim through the opening. He played his light into the plane, getting the first look inside the cockpit at what might very well be the most sought-after missing aircraft in the world.

Bones echoed his thoughts as he leveled out next him in front of the windscreen. "No bodies that I can see."

"Right. Shall we?" Maddock extended a hand into the cockpit.

"Ladies first."

It was a tight squeeze, but Maddock floated through the opening into the Electra's cockpit, descending between the two steering wheels, one in front of each of the two cockpit seats. Looking down as he passed over, he saw that the instrument console was encrusted with growth, although mostly still readable. Looking aft, toward the tail of the plane, he found he could see all the way to the end of it as it passed through the coral wall on the outside. Jumbles of gear and debris littered the interior of the fuselage. He could see right away that it would take some time to sort out.

"Man, they weren't much for legroom back in the day, were they?" Bones settled in between the pilot and co-pilots' seats on the floor of the plane, right behind Maddock.

"Amelia was quite a bit shorter than you. Better looking, too."

"You got me there. Plus the navigator guy, Noonan—he sat in back with all his equipment, so this front seat was unoccupied." He tapped the rim of the seat, sending a puff of silt wafting into the water.

"Hey, somebody read up on their history. I'm impressed!" Maddock was careful not to reference their briefing documents. "Now let's get to work. Serial number. Should be a small brass plate up here. Pilot's side under the console."

Bones turned around and positioned himself so that he could look underneath the instrument cluster. "Looking..." He directed his beam along the growth-covered surfaces. There was only room for one of them in that area of the plane so Maddock played his light around the rear cargo area while he waited. He saw two globe-shaped objects on either side of the floor. He kicked off and floated gently over to them like an astronaut inside a space station.

"Think I've got it." Bones lay sideways in the cockpit, his head wedged beneath the pilot seat, facing forward. One hand held him in position while the other held his light.

"Think I've got something back here, too." Maddock settled onto his knees next to one of the globular objects. He fanned a gloved hand over it, clearing some of the silt that had accumulated there. Near the base of the object was an opening. He slipped his fingers inside it and lifted. At first nothing happened but he sure it was supposed to be a sliding dome cover, so he pulled again, more forcefully this time, and he was rewarded with a snapping sound as the dome's cover slid open. Beneath it was the other half of the spherical shape—containing a large camera. He could see that, although now nearly opaque with marine growth, the dome was some sort of plastic that was set through the plane's body, enabling pictures to be taken looking straight down.

Odd that if this is Earhart's plane, she would have had it modified to accommodate these kinds of cameras. The extra weight and expense, compromising the integrity of the fuselage...

"Metal plate!" Bones' excited tone shook him from his thoughts.

"Can you read it?"

"Hold on. Let me see if I can scrub it off . Cross your fingers."

Maddock turned around to see Bones in the cockpit. His light was held steady on one spot.

"Yes! Serial number. I can read it. NR—"

"Wait. Hold on, let me write it down." Maddock picked up the writing slate and pencil clipped to his vest. "Go."

"NR 16020."

Maddock wrote down the numbers with mounting excitement until the string was complete. He recognized the serial number from their briefing materials.

They were inside Amelia Earhart's lost airplane!

A flash of light going off up front indicated that Bones took a photo of the plate.

"How's it going back there?" Bones extricated himself from beneath the instrument console and turned around to look at Maddock.

"Found some—" Maddock cut himself off, aware that Watanabe would probably be able to hear him. "Found some stuff back here, not sure what it all is," he settled on. Visually, he made an exaggerated pointing motion toward the dome camera he sat next to. Bones nodded his understanding and swam over. He looked at the camera, then frowned, wagging a hand back and forth as if to say, it was iffy that it was worth anything. The dome port was completely flooded and although it was clear that the object inside had been a camera, it was now little more than a rusted mass of parts fused together. Maddock went to the camera on the other side and examined it. Same thing. When he looked up from it, Bones was pointing at something in the rear of the plane.

A couple of boxes, taking up a fair amount of space. That's what they looked like to Maddock from his position at the ruined dome camera. He and Bones swam through the plane to the rear-most cargo area, passing over what was obviously navigation equipment—brass devices that looked like sextants, a small telescope, a chronometer and a ruler of some type. They ignored them, heading for the boxes. Maddock went to one and Bones the other. Constructed of metal, they were each about two feet on a side. They had stout buckles and looked like they might still have watertight seals. Maddock cleared some twisted metal off his until he could heft its weight. He set it back down after realizing that it would not be easy to move.

He motioned to Bones to get his attention and held a

finger over his lips outside his mask, warning him not to mention the boxes over the comm line. Bones nodded and looked at his air gauge, reminding Maddock to do the same. In their excitement of finding a way inside the plane, both had forgotten to check their air for a while.

The numbers were not encouraging.

"Time to go." Maddock immediately dropped his crate and wrote on his slate, showing it to Bones: NEXT TIME.

Bones nodded.

Maddock quickly took some digital snapshots of the plane's cabin—without showing the boxes—and then he and Bones swam out through the Electra's windshield.

CHAPTER 7

Maddock and Bones climbed into the Zodiac and removed their dive gear while Watanabe motored back to shore. They had seen no signs of the whale despite their wariness. The swim back to the boat had been thankfully uneventful. To their surprise, Watanabe asked them how the dive went, saying that he lost radio contact with them for most of the time they were in the plane, probably because the cave blocked the radio signals. This meant that he didn't yet know they had found the plane's serial number and confirmed it to be that of Earhart's plane. There was no way they could have a conversation in the small boat without Watanabe hearing or at least becoming suspicious, so Maddock thought things through to himself.

He and Bones could keep the discovery of the serial number to themselves and actually fabricate a story that they found some other serial number, meaning it was not Earhart's plane, in the hopes that Spinney would take their word for it and leave the island. Maddock had to suppress a laugh as he realized how unlikely that was. Spinney would never take anyone's word for it when it came to the identification of the plane which had become his life's obsession. They might as well tell the truth and get in Spinney's good graces, then keep diving the site in the company of the EARHART team. They would just have to deal later with how to snoop around the plane without Spinney's divers being any the wiser.

"It's Earhart's plane!" Maddock told Watanabe, who actually slowed the boat to make sure he'd heard him right.

"*What?*"

Maddock repeated himself, adding that they had found the serial number. Watanabe let out a howl of joy that would have made a werewolf jealous. Then he picked up the radio and broke the news to base camp. When they got to the pier, the whole team was waiting for them.

Spinney was the first one to the boat. "Pictures? Did you get any pictures?"

Maddock was surprised to feel a twinge of anger for not being taken at their word, but then realized it was probably for the media. He looked over at Bones and saw that it rankled him, too. But they did in fact have pictures, so the hefty Indian turned on his digital camera and brought the shots of the brass number plate up on the screen, then handed it over to Spinney.

Maddock watched as a grin consumed the EARHART leader's features. The bearded man nodded in exaggerated fashion, as if convincing himself it was real before mentioning it to anyone else.

"We got it!" he said, handing the camera off to his researcher.

Carlson stared at the miniature screen intently. "These are the winning lotto numbers! You know, it's funny. Electra was a prophetic model of plane for Earhart. It was named by Lockheed, as all of their planes of that era were, after a constellation. In this case, for the lost star in the constellation of Pleiades. But now it is lost no more!"

He passed the camera to one of the divers, everyone wanting to see it for themselves, to somehow be a part of the historic event even though they weren't in the water to personally make the discovery. Maddock supposed the fact that the two newcomers had made the big discovery might even become a source of irritation for the divers, and he made a mental note to be aware of that. Their objective was difficult enough without making enemies along the way.

As Maddock passed the camera to one of the divers, he saw the man's eyes look down, to Maddock's waist. Once he took the camera Maddock looked down and realized that the man had been staring at what he had written on his underwater slate during the dive: NEXT TIME. By itself it wasn't incriminating, but it did expose the concept that they were communicating outside of the facemask comm units. Maddock mentally kicked himself for the lapse. He had to remember to erase whatever he wrote before they got back to the boat.

Spinney motioned to Carlson. "Let's get back to camp. What do you think about a press conference announcing we found it?"

Carlson stared past the pier to the dive site beyond while he spoke. "It would have so much more impact if we also found their bodies..." He trailed off while he turned to face Maddock and Bones.

"I assume you didn't find any bodies? No bones?"

The two undercover SEALs both shook their heads and Carlson immediately went back to addressing Spinney. "I think it's worth one more search of the surrounding site to see if anything else can be found." He turned back to Maddock and Bones.

"How did you get into the plane, by the way?"

Maddock explained the tunnel system he and Bones found, and then Carlson continued. "Okay, so it's possible that there are human remains that were washed deep into this tunnel system. The world has waited over sixty years, it can wait another day, right?" He directed this at Spinney, holding his hands palms up as if to say, *it's worth a shot.*

After a moment of what appeared to be genuine deliberation, Spinney nodded. But it looked to Maddock as though the man really wanted to make the announcement right now and claim the fame that he'd been seeking for so long.

"It can wait a half a day. One more dive this afternoon to search the tunnels. If no remains are found, then we contact the media anyway and say that we found Amelia Earhart's plane based solely on the serial number plate. Let's go, people!"

The dive team helped Maddock and Bones grab the gear out of the Zodiac and started back to camp. However, as Maddock fell into stride behind them, he felt Spinney's hand grip his arm.

"You there." Maddock was somehow offended that the man had already forgotten his bogus name, nor did he even ask what it was again. He was literally nothing but an anonymous worker to him.

"You took photos, too?" He pointed to the digital camera dangling from Maddock's weight belt. Maddock nodded, unclipping it and turning it on to display the images. He was glad he hadn't taken any of the crates. He showed Spinney a shot of the exterior cockpit, taken from inside the cave.

Upon looking for the first time at the shots he'd taken, Maddock was surprised to see evidence of 50-caliber strafing near the underside of the nose section, as well as what they saw before near the tail. He made a remark about it to Spinney.

"Yeah, we saw the bullet holes in the tail section." He looked at Maddock and shrugged. "There are theories that Earhart was captured by the Japanese after her plane went down..." He said nothing further, his mind appearing almost hypnotized by the image on the tiny screen. He advanced to the next photo, a wider shot of the front of the plane they accessed via the tunnel system. He furrowed his brow.

"What is it?" Maddock prompted.

Spinney ignored Maddock and called Carlson back over. "Take a look at this. It's the nose section. You notice anything strange?"

He handed Maddock's camera off to his researcher, who held it up close to his face and squinted. He alternately held the camera at arm's length and then right in front of his eyes before handing it back to Spinney. "It's a Lockheed Electra all right, but from this angle it's clearly not a model 10-E, which is what she was supposed to have been flying." He turned to Maddock as he said the last part of the sentence, since he knew Spinney was already aware of this fact. Maddock nodded while Carlson went on.

"It actually looks more like an Electra 12, which was their largest and fastest plane in the Electra line during that period."

Spinney nodded. "Electra 12, that's what I thought."

"Does that mean it might not be her plane?" Maddock

asked, eliciting scowls from both men.

Spinney pushed the camera back into Maddock's hands. "No, that serial number is ironclad proof."

"Especially when combined with this location," Carlson piped in, waving an arm at their surroundings.

Spinney looked at Maddock. "If there's one thing I've learned from looking for this airplane the last thirty years, it's that Amelia Earhart is like a mystery wrapped in a riddle and punched in the face by a conundrum or however the hell that old saying goes."

"Definitely one of the most enduring mysteries of modern times," the researcher added.

"It's why the conspiracy theorists love her. Now we're finally going to set the record straight. Let's go prepare those press releases, Steve!" Then, to Maddock: "Carry on."

He and Carlson left Maddock behind while they started up the path to camp.

CHAPTER 8

That afternoon, Watanabe took the entire dive team—
Maddock and Bones plus Spinney's four divers—out to the
wreck site. Maddock and Bones sat across from each other,
each reading the others' thoughts as they sat amidst the
other men. Retrieving the crates they'd found inside the
plane earlier without anyone else knowing about it was going
to be very difficult.

Once on site the dive team leader reviewed the plan.
Two of Spinney's divers were to search the tunnel system
for bodies or bones, while two more would accompany
Maddock and Bones into the airplane.

A few minutes later the six divers drifted over the coral
lip and onto the ledge where Earhart's plane had sat for over
six decades. Maddock led the way into the tunnel's ceiling
entrance.

"You can go either left or right here," he explained
through the communication units to the two divers who
were charged with searching the tunnels. "Left leads
eventually to the airplane, but with forks along the way, and
right is unknown; we never went that way."

The tunnel team headed off to the right while Maddock
and Bones led the other two divers left and to the airplane's
cockpit chamber. When they dropped into the cavity,
Maddock made a beeline for the plane's windshield. Bones
was only a fin length behind him. They needed to be the
first ones inside the wreck.

"Easiest access looks to be through the windshield,"
Maddock said as he glided through it. The other two divers
treaded water while they assessed the opening and waited for
Maddock and Bones to move deeper into the plane.
Maddock didn't need to tell Bones what they needed to do.

They swam to the rear of the plane and located the two
boxes, in plain sight. Behind them, the first of their two

"associates" entered the cockpit. Maddock looked around and saw a section of metal that had peeled away from the fuselage. He pointed it out to Bones and then worked to curl it over one of the boxes.

He looked toward the cockpit and saw the second diver now entering, the first facing in his direction.

Bones looked around but could find nothing else with which to cover the second crate. The second diver was now inside the cockpit, his partner turning slowly around to face into the cargo hold. Maddock made a rapid, frantic hand motion indicating for Bones to move the second crate closer to the first, right next to it. While Bones moved the crate, Maddock peeled back some more of the metal sheeting that had separated from the plane's body. He pulled it off the side, knowing what Carlson's reaction would be to causing further damage and disturbance to a modern archaeological find of such significance, until the metal covered both crates. Bones pulled the end of it into place, tucking it under the second crate with his gloved hand.

The two strongboxes were now hidden from direct view, but just barely.

The first diver swam into the hold with them. Maddock's heart stopped cold when he asked, "What are those?" Then he saw that he was pointing to the dome cameras. Maddock almost told him it was a camera and then checked himself. He was just supposed to be a run-of-the-mill commercial diver. His false identity had no reason to know about any special equipment Amelia Earhart and Fred Noonan might have been using.

"Got me. I'll take some pictures." He made a show of taking snapshots around the cabin, taking care to avoid the obscured crates. Bones did the same. The second diver knelt at the space between the cockpit and the cargo hold, the rear area not large enough to accommodate all four of them at once.

Maddock pointed out the navigation equipment they'd spotted earlier and unclipped a mesh bag from his belt. "See that sextant and stuff? I'll bag that and bring it up."

Maddock knew that the navigation gear had nothing to do with his mission, and so it would help to bolster his cover if he handed it over to Spinney.

"Definitely. I'll get some of this other stuff." Bones began picking up random odds and ends—loose bolts, small things Maddock couldn't readily identify, corroded tin cans—and put them in a bag of his own. Neither of Spinney's two divers took any pictures, which Maddock was grateful for. They didn't need anyone wondering later on what was going on with that curl of scrap metal back there.

After a couple more minutes of collecting, the diver in back with Maddock and Bones looked at his air pressure gauge and said to his dive buddy in the cockpit, "I'm a thousand psi. How about you?"

"Nine hundred. We should go." Maddock knew he was right. The team had an agreed-upon minimum reading of one thousand psi air at this depth. If they didn't have more than that, they had to return to the surface.

"What about you guys?" He looked into Maddock's eyes through his mask. Maddock brought the gauge up to his face, catching a stare of caution from Bones as he did so. The question was not as simple as it seemed. More experienced divers used less air. This was because they were more comfortable in the water and knew proper breathing techniques and swimming methods to conserve energy and air consumption. He and Bones weren't supposed to be more experienced than these guys. Equal, maybe, but not more.

Maddock's gauge read 1,800. "I have one thousand, three-hundred," he told the diver.

"Twelve-hundred here." The big Cherokee would use more air than the smaller Maddock, so this reading made sense.

"Wow, I'm guessing you two guys aren't smokers?" The other of Spinney's divers laughed.

Maddock and Bones both said that they weren't.

"Okay, well John and I are going to head up to the deco stop and do our hang time. We'll see you on the boat."

Maddock and Bones knew that he meant they were going to ascend to a shallower depth in order to avoid decompression sickness before surfacing.

"See you in a few." Maddock studiously snapped off a couple of more pictures while Spinney's two divers exited the plane through the cockpit window.

"Here comes the tunnel team," the diver said about a minute after leaving the plane. He called out to Maddock and Bones by their cover names. "All four of us heading up now. See you on the boat."

"Copy that." Maddock immediately wrote something on his slate, pointed at the crates, and showed what he had written to Bones.

Take them to reef.

Drop there. Pick up tonight.

Bones nodded. It was a plan that might just work. This was the last dive of the day for everyone. If they left the boxes on the shallow reef flat at the top of the wall, near the boat, they could do an easy and quick dive tonight to retrieve them before anyone else was the wiser. Bones moved to the crates and peeled back the sheet metal that had so far prevented them from being seen.

Manhandling the heavy boxes through the plane and out the windshield was not as easy as they'd hoped. It took Maddock and Bones a lot of effort to get just one of the boxes outside the plane. They knew that from there they'd have to maneuver it through the tunnels back out to the ledge. That meant if any of Spinney's divers should come back down to the ledge for any reason, they would see it.

They swam back to the remaining crate. It was even heavier than the first. Maddock consulted his air gauge. Now he really *was* down to 1,300 psi. The heavy exertion of wrestling with the boxes was taking its toll. Plus they would have to do some extra swimming up on the shallow reef to dump the box before going to the boat. He gave Bones a thumbs up, the signal to ascend. Bones glanced at his own pressure gauge and nodded. He pulled the metal back into place over the crate they would have to leave in the plane.

The SEAL duo swam out of the plane through the windshield and up into the tunnel with the crate. Bones shoveled the crate ahead of him through the tunnels, guided by Maddock. A few minutes later, they came out in the cavern under the ledge where the main body of the plane stuck through the coral wall. Reaching the tail section, they looked around for signs of the other divers but thankfully couldn't see any.

Maddock pointed to the lift bag, a device used in underwater salvage operations consisting of a large, heavy-duty bag that could be filled with air from a scuba regulator, clipped to Bones' belt, indicating that they should use it to lift the crate.

Bones set to work preparing the webbing harness of the bag while Maddock pushed the box into position. When they had it set in the harness, Bones took the regulator mouthpiece from his mouth and used it to inflate the lift bag. As the bag began to fill, slowly lifting the box from where it rested on the ledge, Maddock guided it off the ledge and clear of the overhang.

With the box suspended in open water, as if floating in a void, Maddock and Bones began their ascent. Bones was careful to regulate the speed of the rising lift bag. Air expanded as it rose to shallower depths, and he had to occasionally vent air from the bag or it would rise too fast and get away from them. If they lost control of it, the rig could shoot to the surface without them where the other divers on the boat would see it.

They reached the top of the wall and the shallow coral flat, where the outline of the boat was visible above. Maddock considered their options. Their bubbles would be visible to those in the boat now. He decided to make communication with the team. Remaining quiet after so long might be suspicious.

"We're making our deco stop," he announced.

Watanabe's voice came back. "Copy that. You have artifacts, right? Spinney's already asking about what we found."

Bones smirked as he eyed the hanging box. Maddock glanced at the mesh bag clipped to his belt loaded with the navigation gear.

"Yeah, we got some good stuff—navigation equipment, I think, but I'm not sure—and some photos."

"Roger. See you in a few."

Maddock pointed out across the flat reef, away from the boat. Bones nodded and they began moving, with Maddock swimming slightly above the bag to block its yellow material from being seen by the team while they were close to the boat. It might seem a little odd that they were moving around during their decompression stop instead of remaining in one place, as was the norm, but as long as one stayed at a constant, suitable depth, there was nothing wrong with it.

In fact, Maddock thought, as he spotted a pair of antennae sticking out from under a coral formation, he could think of a good reason for doing it. He swam at an angle toward the lobster, careful not to spook it. When he saw it start to crawl backward into the coral, though, he knew it was alerted to his presence, so he backed off and circled around. Bones held his hands up in a *what are you doing?* gesture, and Maddock pointed at the lobster. If he could catch it, it would present the perfect excuse for wanting to swim around over the reef during the decompression stop.

Maddock swam over the top of a bulbous brain coral four feet in diameter and descended head first to just above the spot where the lobster continued its retreat, hoping to surprise it. The tactic worked. The "bug," as divers called them, had walked further away from the coral out onto the open sand. Maddock stopped, poised above the sloping brain coral. He would have to move fast and decisively or the bug would retreat into its coral haven and not come out again.

He took a deep breath, held it for a second while he watched the invertebrate stop walking, and then he sprang. With a powerful kick of his fins, Maddock closed on the

DAVID WOOD AND RICK CHESLER | 68

creature, trapping it firmly in the sand with both hands. He felt its powerful tail muscles working as it tried to flee but he maintained a firm grip with his gloved hands until he was able to drop it into the same mesh bag that held the Earhart artifacts.

He caught up with Bones, who was still dragging the lift bag across the reef. They were now a safe distance from the boat, but not so far away that the site would be difficult to find later. Still, their return would be at night, so Maddock looked around for any kind of distinctive terrain or landmarks they could use as a reference point. He spotted a thick cluster of branching Elkhorn coral in the midst of an otherwise sandy patch and decided that it would have to do.

He pointed it out to Bones, who nodded and released the air from the lift bag so that it dropped onto the sand next to the bright yellow formation. As Maddock swam up to Bones, he spotted another lobster, this one positioned for an easy grab. He scooped it up and dropped it into the bag. Bones gave him a big grin, and then pointed back toward the boat. It was time to go.

The pair of SEALs traveled across the reef until they were directly under the waiting Zodiac. They slowly swam to the surface, where the divers were waiting to grab their gear as they came up. When Maddock put his head back into the water to remove his fins, he saw something below.

Something sleek and dark was moving toward them from out of the depths. Moving fast.

CHAPTER 9

"Go! Get in the boat!" Maddock yelled at Bones, who was right next to him in the water, one hand on the boat's pontoon. Through his mask, he saw Bones wince at the loud voice coming out of his earpiece.

"What's up?" Bones looked around and saw nothing. He started to look into the water.

"Don't look. Just go!" Maddock reached a hand out to a diver in the boat whose eyes widened at the sight of whatever was coming at them from below. He reached a strong arm out and began to haul Maddock in while another diver reached out to Bones. Maddock's chest was up on the boat's pontoon when they felt the impact.

They heard shouts of "Whale!" at the same time the Zodiac lifted partially into the air, tipping up on one side before splashing back down. They heard a sharp hissing of air.

"Did you see that? He punctured the tube!" a diver said.

"Patch it up with duct tape!" Watanabe instructed.

Meanwhile, Maddock and Bones had slid off the boat back into the water, where they now stared into the depths.

"I see it." Maddock's voice was low and steady. "Pilot whale. It's got a blade strapped to its snout."

"Slashed our boat!" Watanabe said.

"Here he comes again," Bones warned. He didn't try getting back into the boat again. "We're sitting ducks up here." He jerked his thumb downward to indicate they should drop down to the bottom. Maddock nodded in agreement and they vented the air from their buoyancy vests, sinking back below the waves while the boat crew struggled to patch the inflatable boat before it flooded and sank.

Maddock sized up the animal on their way back down to the reef. It was a small whale, about as long as two of the dolphins they'd just finished training with, but with a lot more girth. So it was much bigger overall, but at least there was only one of them. Regardless of the whale's size, the knife on its rostrum left no doubt as to the purpose of the beast's training. This was no exercise where they would be "tagged." It had been sent to deal out some serious damage, perhaps even kill.

Bones held a finger from each hand together, repeating the signal Maddock had used in the training exercise. Dane agreed. If the two of them separated, the whale could attack them individually and the other wouldn't be of much help. They moved into the back-to-back formation, assuming a standing position on the bottom. The whale slowed and cruised around them in a circle, sunlight dancing off its blade.

"Looks like a bayonet," Maddock said. There was no need for radio silence now. The entire team was battling the pilot whale, and the conversation would stick to that. He cautioned himself not to reference any of their dolphin training experiences aloud, though.

Bones spoke into his facemask. "How's that boat repair going?"

"We're pumping air back into it now to see if it holds. You guys okay?" Watanabe sounded stressed.

Maddock kept a sharp eye on the whale as he spoke. "We're on the bottom. The whale is keeping its distance for now, but circling around us. When you get the boat ready let us know and we'll make a beeline for it."

"Will do. Stand by."

Maddock glimpsed a flash of metal in his peripheral vision, even though the whale was in front of him. He looked back and saw Bones holding his dive knife at the ready. He hoped Boens could strike swiftly enough, should the whale try and ram them. When he bent down to release his own blade from its sheath, he saw the mesh bag on his belt and got an idea.

The lobsters! When it came time to swim to the surface, they would be very exposed to a hit by the whale. Right now at least they had the bottom under their feet, so they couldn't be attacked from that direction. He knew that small toothed whales were fond of eating crustaceans, including lobsters. So perhaps if he let the bugs go they might provide a distraction long enough for him and Bones to get into the boat.

"I've got an idea," he announced to Bones, and of course, the team who were monitoring the comm channel.

"Uh-oh." In spite of the situation, Bones grinned behind his facemask.

"What is it?" Watanabe wanted to know. "Boat's holding air. We're ready when you are. I'll have the engine running in neutral."

They heard the outboard motor crank to life, its whiny rumble clearly audible down on the reef. In response, the whale emitted a series of clicks that increased in pitch and cadence.

"Copy that. I caught a couple of lobsters down here on the reef during our deco stop."

He heard a couple of the divers burst into laughter. Watanabe returned, "We were wondering what you guys were doing swimming around down there."

"What can I say? I love my seafood. Anyway, I can let these bugs go, and hopefully the whale will chase after them. From what I hear, this breed of whale won't turn its nose down at a free snack."

"We're ready up here. Just tell us when you're coming up. We'll have you in the boat faster than a fat kid grabbing a cookie."

"Hey, I resent that," Bones said. "I was a fat kid before I discovered girls and got all studly."

Watanabe came back. "You guys ever worry about anything? Catching lobsters, cracking jokes...there's a whale trying to kill us. And you're the ones in the water."

"It's called denial," Maddock replied. He watched the pilot whale reach the outer arc of its circle. He opened his bag and pulled out both of the lobsters, one in each hand, while making sure the bag was securely closed, lest the artifacts drop out. That would not sit well with anyone, especially Spinney.

"Keith." He gave Bones a light elbow to the back. "I need you to close my bag. My hands are full." He waved the pair of lobsters. Bones reached around and did the clasp on Maddock's bag.

"You're good to go."

"Let's do it." He saw Bones turn his head to watch him. "On three..."

The whale gradually closed the distance between them as it circled around.

"One..." Maddock shifted the lobster in his right hand so that when he released it, it would scoot toward the whale. At least that was the plan.

"Two..." They heard Watanabe instructing the divers in the boat to get into position.

"Three!" Maddock released the lobster with a flick of his wrist. The beleaguered crustacean floated there for a second, then began a series of rapid tail flips, propelling itself away from Maddock and Bones and toward the whale.

Maddock and Bones pushed hard off the bottom, separating as they began to kick rapidly for the boat.

"Go!" Maddock doubted Bones really needed any encouragement, but it couldn't hurt and it would let the boat crew know they were on the way. Looking over his shoulder, Maddock watched the pilot whale scoop up the lobster and crush it with its rows of widely-spaced serrated teeth. So much for that. Now the beast tilted upward, eyeing them momentarily before launching itself towards the fleeing divers. Maddock and Bones were about half way to the boat, another fifteen feet to go.

Maddock dropped his other lobster, grateful that it chose to zigzag crazily in the whale's general direction, no doubt catching its attention. The whale abruptly changed direction, chasing after the second lobster while Maddock and Bones continued their beeline for the Zodiac. Once again, though, Maddock was shocked to see just how effective a hunter the pilot whale was, sucking the crustacean into its open maw before it even reached the bottom.

"He's got the last bug. Go, go!" Maddock urged them on the final feet to the boat. He no longer looked down, but knew the whale would be coming for them as soon as the lobster slid down its gullet. He and Bones saw the blurry shapes of the divers leaning over the boat to help them in as they rushed up to the surface.

They burst from the water at the same time, both of them landing halfway in the boat. The pilot whale reached the boat at almost the same time. It slashed its bayonet across the back of Bones' calf just as several pairs of hands hauled him into the boat. They pulled Maddock in the same way. Moments later, the two SEALs lay, breathing heavily, on the bottom of the Zodiac.

Watanabe put the motor in gear before the whale could make another pass, gunning it for the island. Maddock pushed himself up and looked over the side of the boat. The pilot whale followed in their wake for a bit, jumping the waves, but after a few minutes it fell back.

Maddock rose to his knees and made a quick inspection of Bones' injury.

"What's it look like?" Bones asked.

"Not deep at all. I'll bandage it up and you should be healed in time for swimsuit season." He cleaned the wound and wrapped it in clean gauze.

"Nice work. You should have been a nurse. The uniform would suit you."

Watanabe laughed, but his mirth soon vanished. He pointed off to his left, where the white ship was visible, perhaps a mile away. "Mizuhi!" he called out over the whine of the outboard. The men spoke angrily about the Japanese conglomerate until they docked at the pier, where Spinney and Carlson were waiting, arms crossed.

"Trouble?" Spinney looked down on the general state of disarray the boat was in, including salt water mixed with Bones' blood from the gash in his calf sluicing around the boat. He listened to the excited chatter of his divers as they offloaded the gear onto the pier.

Watanabe responded while he shut down the motor. "Mizuhi's at it again." He told him about the pilot whale and the ship.

Spinney shook his head as if in sympathy, but then quickly added, "How'd the dive go? Recover anything?"

Bugsy, his lead diver, stepped up onto the pier. "We searched the tunnel system but found no human remains, Mr. Spinney. We did recover artifacts from the plane." He glanced back at Maddock and Bones, who were handing the gear up out of the boat to two other divers on the pier. Spinney whistled in their direction, waving an arm to come over.

Maddock looked up and gave him a hard stare. If he wasn't undercover he would not put up with this kind of treatment, but to anger the man meant jeopardizing their mission, so he shoved the feelings aside.

"Let's see what you got," Spinney called. Maddock and Bones brought their artifact bags over to Spinney, Carlson and Bugsy.

"Mine looks like navigation equipment, from the cargo area," Maddock said, handing the bag over to Spinney's eager hands.

Carlson nodded. "That's the space where Fred Noonan sat. Wasn't enough room in the co-pilot seat for all his gear, so he rode back there."

"And you?" Spinney eyed Bones' bag, which he handed over without a word.

He took a cursory look at some of the stuff and closed the bags, holding onto them. He turned to Carlson and said, "Okay, so no bodies, but we've got more artifacts. Let's get back to camp and catalog these. Hopefully there's something definitively linked to Earhart in here, then we can make our press release."

Carlson nodded.

"Big night!" Spinney enthused. He started to turn away and then spun back around. "Oh, Bugsy said you took photos? May I see?" He held out his meaty hand. Maddock called up the shots he'd taken on the device's screen and handed it to him.

"Got several inside the cargo area this time." Maddock watched him as he scrolled through the images, clearly fascinated. Then he looked up at Bones. "You too?"

Bones handed over his camera.

"You two mind if we take these back to camp and transfer the files to the field computer?"

Maddock and Bones both shook their heads. They had been careful not to take pictures that would compromise their mission. They would prefer Spinney didn't scrutinize them too carefully, but it wasn't worth creating a scene over.

"Rest of the day off," Spinney said to Maddock and Bones as he and Carlson started up the path. The dive team would need a long topside rest in order to avoid the bends. The undercover SEALs fell back in with the dive team and carried the gear back into camp.

CHAPTER 10

Maddock and Bones finished off the last of their fish dinners and set their plates aside. Spinney, Carlson, their radioman, Sims, and the Australian photographer, George Taylor, had retreated to the research tent earlier, where they worked on the artifacts and press release. Spinney had been discussing possible titles for the media release all night, and so far, his favorite seemed to be, "Fred Spinney's EARHART Group finds the Lost Airplane of Amelia Earhart in the Phoenix Islands." Spinney and his associates were still arguing about it when they left. Without them at dinner, the divers had enjoyed a lively recounting of the day's events.

"Too bad, no lobster for supper tonight, eh boys?" Bugsy joked, cracking up the team. The topic of conversation around that night's campfire dinner had been a steady diet of Mizuhi and their trained pilot whale. The divers rehashed the events of the day in detail, exaggerating some things, underplaying others, depending on who was telling the story and how it made them look, but all agreed on one thing: "Mizuhi's not going to stop until they kill somebody," Bugsy summarized.

"I wonder how safe it will be to dive tomorrow," mused another.

Bugsy shrugged and said, "We know now that if the ship is as close as it was today, that's within striking distance for their whale. So if we see it there tomorrow, we could decide to call off the dive." He lowered his voice. "We could ask Spinney to call Mizuhi on the radio and come to some kind of truce before we get wet again."

"And if he says no, he won't call?" one of the divers who had been inside the plane with Maddock and Bones asked.

Joking, but softly called cries of "Mutiny, mutiny,

mutiny..." rang out around the fire.

"We'll just have to see how it goes tomorrow. Get a good night's sleep is what I advise." Bugsy stood and stretched, then headed off to his tent. Spinney's other three divers remained talking, but Maddock and Bones excused themselves shortly after Bugsy left and walked to the tent they shared. Inside the shelter, Maddock spoke at a near-whisper to Bones.

"I think we should talk to somebody who knows something more than we do about Amelia Earhart." He grabbed his backpack and from it removed the satellite phone given to them by their mission handlers.

"Like who?" Bones eyed the phone with concern. "That's military property, encrypted and for mission use only."

"Since when do you care about things like that?"

Bones shrugged. "Since never. I just wanted to see what it feels like to be you. It's boring."

Maddock rolled his eyes. "This *is* for mission use. I don't understand what's going on with this plane. Spinney and Carlson say that it's not the same model that Earhart flew. But the serial number is the same."

"What? You mean it might not be the right plane? Dude, you know how I feel about doing work for nothing."

Maddock sighed. "I don't know. I only know that I heard Spinney and Carlson say that the plane down there is an Electra model 12, while Earhart should have been flying an Electra model 10E."

"And there are the bullet holes."

Maddock looked over at Bones, whispering sharply. "Right! But..." He broke off, lost in thought.

"But what?"

"That part of it might make some sense, because...why are we here?"

"To find Earhart's plane," Bones said.

"Well yeah, but more specifically?"

"To bring certain things from the plane back to the Navy."

"Bingo! Film. And smallpox canisters. To the military. And we did find those weird cameras. All of which suggests some kind of military involvement."

"Okay, that could explain the 50-cal damage, if she flew into a war zone. But what about the plane being the wrong model?"

Maddock turned the sat-phone over in his hands. "I just don't know. Maybe Spinney and Carlson are wrong and it is a 10E? Maybe they're right and she really did fly a different model that wasn't publicized, because it would have been considered cheating or not as impressive a feat? Or maybe it's just not her airplane."

"Another Electra from the same time period that just happened to crash in this part of the world?" Doubt filled Bones' face.

"What I don't like about this whole thing from an information-gathering standpoint is that we're in the middle of two biased parties. Spinney and his group want to believe more than anything that they've found Earhart's plane. The realization of a long-time goal could be clouding their judgment. On the other hand, it's in the Navy's best interest to compartmentalize what they know and only tell us the bare minimum of what we need in order to accomplish our mission objectives."

Bones nodded. "The commander about told us as much in the briefing."

Maddock looked at the sat-phone. "So I'd like to talk to a neutral party who knows something about Earhart and might be able to fill in some details for us. Who do we know that would be good for that?"

It didn't take Bones long to come up with an answer. "Jimmy Letson?"

A smile overtook Maddock's features while he thought about this. Letson was an ex-Navy man who now worked as a reporter in the Boston area. He was knowledgeable about a lot of things, especially those involving conspiracies, and he was good with computers. From time to time they'd asked him to look things up for them and found him to be good at it, although he always expected something in return, usually a quality bottle of liquor.

Maddock rummaged through his pack until he found his address book. "Let's give him a call, but not here. Outside camp."

They exited the tent and strolled through the outer perimeter of the campsite, avoiding the research tent and the other sleeping tents. They passed the dive tent, where the compressor was now silent, their tanks having been refilled earlier in the day. At one end, they came to a sandy trail that led down to the lagoon-side beach. Exotic birdcalls punctuated the evening while a half-moon cast its silvery light across the atoll's lagoon.

They took the few steps down from the slightly elevated base camp to the beach, then walked for a while up the sandy strip until they came to a palm tree leaning out over the sand. Deciding they were now suitably far out of earshot from the team, Maddock leaned against the tree and activated the sat-phone.

"What time is it in Boston?" Bones asked. "I can't keep track of this time zone crap."

"Late. But it's not like he keeps regular hours." Maddock shrugged.

"What" came the curt answer on the other end of the line.

"Jimmy, it's Maddock. I know it's late, but do you have a few minutes? I'm with Bones and we need a favor."

Letson's voice sounded tinny but audible coming through the speaker from thousands of miles away.

"You still have my address?"

"Yeah, but we're not in the neighborhood, we're in the field—sorry, can't say where—just want to chat."

"I don't want to see you, either, I just want to make sure you know where to send my Chivas Regal."

"We made good on the last one, didn't we?"

"Yeah, that space capsule thing. You just can't do anything without my help, can you?"

"I guess not. So listen. What we have going on here is

even more so. We need to clarify some things. You ready for this?"

"Yeah, go ahead. Been up working on a deadline, so the two most important machines to my existence, the coffee maker and the computer, are both fired up. What do you need?"

"We have questions about Amelia Earhart, especially the type of plane she was flying when she disappeared."

There was a pause on the other end of the line. Maddock watched as Bones, who couldn't hear the other end of the conversation, occupied himself with maintaining watch, head on a swivel as he surveyed their surroundings for signs of anyone coming their way.

Letson barked a laugh. *"Funny. You don't have anything better to do than call and mess with he because I did a magazine article about a year ago on Earhart. I'll have you know, that was some serious journalism. I spent…"*

"Jimmy! Focus!" Maddock said. "We really do want some intel on Earhart."

"Oh." Jimmy sounded surprised.

"So what can you tell us about the plane? Was it an Electra 10E?"

"Yes, yes, that's right. Well, it's half right…" He trailed off.

"Don't mean to rush you, Jimmy, but we're deep in the field and I'm not sure how long my sat-phone battery's going to last."

"Ungrateful as always." Nevertheless, Letson began speaking rapidly. *"Right, so officially, on her round-the-world flight during which she and her navigator disappeared, she was supposed to have been flying a 10E. And on the first attempt, she definitely was. But…"*

"Hold up. Did you say *first* attempt? As in, she tried the round-the-world trip more than once?"

"First you tell me to hurry, then you interrupt me. Make up your mind, Maddock. But, yes, that's correct. Let me lay it out for you. The first trip was definitely in an Electra 10E. She left from San Francisco, flying west, with her first pit-stop in Honolulu."

"Okay…"

"During the takeoff in Honolulu, she had an accident, what pilots

call a "ground loop," where she crashed while still on the runway. Nobody got hurt but the plane was pretty messed up and they had to crate it up and send it back to California for repairs at the Lockheed factory."

"I'm surprised to hear she crashed."

"Eh, it wasn't the first time. Thing about Earhart was, she wasn't really a crack pilot, you know? She was more of a daredevil type. She admitted herself that she didn't fully understand how to operate all of the electronic equipment aboard the plane when she left, although it's probably because there were last minute equipment substitutions made."

"Go on..."

"So some funny things happened in the two months between the Honolulu incident and her second attempt."

Maddock's heart raced. "Like what?"

Letson paused for a second during which Maddock could hear waves breaking out on the reef. "She tried again from San Francisco, but this time there was no announcement made, no big media fanfare. She was married to the publisher, George Putnam, who was also her manager and very big on promotion. He really knew how to pimp her out to the public—female pilot breaking a new record and all that...She did lots of 'em: first Atlantic crossing, first California to Honolulu, an altitude record... After a while the only one left was the equatorial circumnavigation of the globe—by far the most difficult. Anyway, on the second round-the-world attempt, nothing was announced until she popped up in Miami and said, 'Here I am! Going around the world again! Started from San Francisco, so I'm already three thousand miles into it!'"

"That's odd."

"Absolutely. But what's even more strange is the direction of the new flight."

"West-to-east?"

"Exactly. The first attempt was east-to-west, as one would expect for an equatorial circumnavigation that time of year, since that's the direction that will give you the least wind resistance."

"But she didn't go that way."

"Nope."

"Why not?"

Letson took a deep breath before continuing. *"To understand the answer you need to be aware of some of the so-called conspiracy theories that surround Earhart's final flight."*

"Lay it on me."

"Okay. A lot of people think that Earhart was enlisted by Franklin Delano Roosevelt as a spy. Some rumors even have it that Earhart was captured by the Japanese and later forced to become one of the 'Tokyo Rose' radio broadcasters—English speaking women delivering Japanese propaganda to American troops. But anyway, because she would be flying over the Japanese-held regions of the Pacific, FDR wanted her to take photographs of any evidence of military buildup she saw there. She would also be flying over the desert regions of Northern Africa, where there was military buildup occurring as well, but the Pacific was the big gem."

Despite the tropical air, Maddock felt a chill shoot down his spine as he pictured the rusted dome cameras in the Electra out on the reef. Maddock was speechless as he contemplated this, so Letson went on.

"There's more. A lot of people assert that the airplane Earhart took off in from Miami was not an Electra 10E, but was actually an Electra 12, and a heavily modified 12 at that. Extra fuel tanks, bigger engines... So this thing could fly substantially farther, faster and higher than the original Lockheed Electra that she and Putnam bought with their own money."

The skin on Maddock's arms began to crawl as he recalled Spinney looking at his pictures. *Electra 12...*

"And that's another thing: money. This second Electra had absolutely no record of Earhart or Putnam—by the way, do you like how even though she was married to a successful guy she still kept her own name, in the 1930s—that's women's lib for you, right? Anyway, there was no record of her or Putnam buying it. No manifest, invoice, work order, receipt, nothing. Nada"

"Because the military paid for it and gave it to her?"

"Finally, the slow learner begins to catch on! The military also seems to have provided her with fuel, oil and even infrastructure, such as the runway they built for her on Howland Island, all for what was supposedly a civilian operation? But there's even more to it than that."

"I'm all ears."

"The reverse direction only makes sense from a military standpoint. Because weather-wise, it sucks going west-to-east. Not only are you bucking a headwind the entire way, you also hit the monsoon season over in India, which she did and nearly crashed into the Indian Ocean. But from an espionage standpoint, it's great."

"Why?"

"Because if you're spying, you want to carry evidence of that spying—I'm talking about film—with you for the shortest possible time. They accomplish that going west-to-east rather than the other way by hitting the most important war theater, the South and Central Pacific, last. A lot of the countries she had to pass over weren't exactly friendly and only grudgingly granted temporary airspace visas. If they went east-to-west, on the other hand, they'd have to do the spying soon after leaving from Honolulu, a major media stop, by the way, where everyone would see the new plane and possibly notice the modifications made to it at the very beginning of the trip. Then they'd have to schlep that highly sensitive spy film in and out of various customs stops the whole rest of the way around the world."

Maddock was floored. "Wow. So, was Earhart a spy?"

"I don't have a Magic Eight Ball, Maddock. But if I did, it would read: Signs point to yes.*"*

CHAPTER 11

Maddock pulled back the flap of their tent and peeked outside. Quiet, dark, no signs of human activity. He whispered to Bones, "Clear. To the dive tent."

Bones followed him out of the tent and they walked casually but quietly through the camp. If anyone were to see them at this point, they would simply say they were going to take a leak. They reached the dive tent and loaded one of the wheelbarrows with two sets of SCUBA gear and a lift bag. After checking the area again for signs of people, Maddock set out in front as a scout while Bones wheeled the cart. Were they to be seen with the gear, their situation would be very difficult to explain and likely raise suspicions no matter what they said.

They made it down to the pier without any trouble and loaded the gear into the inflatable boat. Maddock checked and was relieved to see that it had been patched more professionally since the duct tape repair out on the water. It appeared to be holding air. He eyed the boat's motor, then looked over toward camp, shaking his head.

"Too much noise to use the outboard. We'll have to paddle." He glanced at the two emergency oars on either side of the boat. Bones nodded and picked one up.

"Just like the good old' days in BUDS!"

For the two Navy SEALs, the physical exertion of the paddle was not a factor. Even after what they had been through, they could do it as easily as walking a block down the street. They would have preferred to get to the site faster, though, but it was not worth the risk of being heard.

They cast off from the pier, Maddock and Bones on opposite sides of the boat, paddling in sync toward the marker buoy at the edge of the reef. The water in the lagoon was so calm and still that by the light of the half-moon they could see individual corals on the sea bottom as they passed over in the boat. About fifteen minutes later they reached the marker buoy and dropped anchor.

They quickly donned their gear, doing a quick check to make sure it was all working properly. They made it a point to deactivate the comm units. They doubted anyone would be monitoring the channel in the middle of the night, but they had no way of knowing for sure and it wasn't worth the risk. They would just have to make do with the old-fashioned way, hand signals. Bones grabbed the lift bag and clipped it to his belt. Ready to make the dive, he scanned the water around them.

"No sign of the whale."

Maddock looked out at the ocean. "I don't see the Mizuhi ship, either, but they could just be leaving their lights off to black themselves out." A ship any distance away without navigation or anchor lights, even a large one, was extremely difficult to spot on the water at night, even in the light of a half-moon.

"Let's do it. Quiet." Bones dangled over the boat's pontoons and slid into the water rather than tumbling in backward, to avoid making a loud splash. Maddock followed suit and then gave the thumbs down signal to descend. They dropped down the thirty feet to the reef, switching their dive lights on only when they had reached the bottom lest they be seen from the beach.

Maddock consulted the compass on his wrist and pointed off to their left. He and Bones swam in that direction, finning quickly over the same brain corals and Staghorn coral formations they'd seen during the day. The reef life was different at night; there were not as many fish swimming about, but they spotted some not usually found in the day. Lots of lobsters now scuttled about in the open, too, Maddock noticed, but there was no reason to grab one now.

After a few more minutes of rapid swimming, they still weren't seeing the crate, only the undersea garden of the reef with its towering corals and meandering patches of sand. Maddock watched as a jellyfish pulsed across his field of vision, dragging behind a trailing mass of stinging tentacles. The water was so clear they could see the moon in the sky from down here, so being able to see wasn't the problem. For one heart-stopping moment, Maddock considered that maybe someone found it—either Bugsy or one of his divers, or perhaps even Mizuhi? Had the whale alerted them to its presence? It was the kind of thing they could be trained to do, and clearly they had put some effort into training it.

But then Bones jiggled his light beam, indicating he saw something up ahead. Maddock also shone his beam on the same spot. There, across a wider sandy patch and next to an isolated branching coral formation...

The crate!

They kicked over to it. As they dropped down in front of it, a large moray eel slithered out from beneath the box and darted between Maddock and Bones and off into open water, startling the two Naval warriors.

They shook it off and got to work. As before, Maddock helped Bones position the crate into the lift bag's web of netting, and then Bones used his regulator to fill the bag with air. When it hung suspended in the water, dangling a few feet above the bottom, Maddock checked his compass, orienting himself. Then he pointed in the direction of the boat and he helped Bones drag the lift bag rig over the reef. The going was slow compared to free swimming, but they made steady progress without stopping, and about ten minutes later, they came to the buoy line.

Maddock looked up and saw the dark outline of the Zodiac at anchor. They ascended, surfaced near the boat, and swam over to it. Maddock removed his gear and got in first. He then assisted Bones with wrangling the heavy crate into the boat, followed by Bones' gear.

Bones pulled in the anchor and they paddled the boat back across the lagoon. When they neared the shore they paused, watching and listening for signs of activity. Detecting none, they sculled the rest of the way to the pier and tied up the Zodiac in the same position in which they had found it, facing out to the lagoon. Maddock made it a point to re-enable the communications units so it didn't have to be done in full view of anyone tomorrow.

They loaded the dive gear and crate into the wheelbarrow and trundled it to the foot of the pier. They had just stepped onto the beach when they heard a voice coming from the shadows.

"Step away from the crate, mates!"

CHAPTER 12

Maddock and Bones froze, looking around for the source of the voice. It had an Australian accent, though, which told Maddock immediately who it was. Suddenly a man rose from a nearby bush. He shone a flashlight from a cupped hand on the pistol he held in his other hand.

"Doing a little moonlighting, are we, boys?"

George Taylor, the topside photographer, stared at Maddock and Bones with a lopsided grin. Maddock and Bones remained silent.

"Decided the pay for this gig sorta sucks compared to selling some Amelia Earhart memorabilia, did we? Can't say as I blame you, especially with our friend Shankey the Whale out there guarding the place. Spinney ought to be giving us hazard pay, right? But listen up: I could give a shout right now and have the gang come running, have ole Spinney perform a citizen's arrest, take you to Honolulu, and turn you in to the police for theft. Or else you let me share in the spoils. I know exactly what you're after."

Silence from Maddock and Bones, save for the soft patter of water dripping from their bodies onto the sand. The Aussie lifted his hands in an oh-come-on-now gesture. "The stamps!"

Maddock and Bones returned genuinely confused looks, but still said nothing.

"Don't play dumb with me. You mean to say you really know nothing about the postal stamps?"

"I haven't collected stamps since I was a kid," Bones said.

The Aussie gave an exasperated sigh, looked briefly around, and addressed Maddock and Bones once more without lowering his weapon. "It's well documented that Earhart had a bunch of first-issue postage stamps brought with her on the flight to have cancelled at local post offices whenever she got a chance during her stops at different countries around the globe. That strongbox looks like it might still be watertight. And if it is, and those stamps happen to be in there—you know what they're worth?"

Maddock and Bones shook their heads, both keeping a sharp eye on Taylor's gun hand.

"Sure you don't. But I happen to know it'd be about twenty-five million U.S. bucks! And I want a piece of it. So go on, to hell with Spinney's archaeological procedures...open the damn crate."

He aimed his light on the box atop the wheelbarrow before directing it back into the faces of Maddock and Bones.

Bones pointed at the dive knife strapped to his calf. "It's rusted shut pretty good after all this time underwater. You mind if I use my dive knife?"

Taylor flicked his light on Bones' blade, which gleamed under its illuminating glow. Then he switched the beam over to Maddock, who carried a similar knife.

"*Real* slow."

Bones walked over to the crate, knife in hand. He eyed the box, hesitating while Maddock looked on.

"Go on, then, let's have a look-see," Taylor prodded.

Bones brought his blade to the lid of the box.

Heavily encrusted with decades' worth of marine growth, it took Bones some time to work it open with his dive knife, crushing the various barnacles and worms out of the way from three sides of the box. Then he started to pry the lid open with the tip of his blade. Still, it stuck.

Maddock worried that Bones might be applying too much force to the container, knowing that it could possibly hold the weaponized smallpox the Commander had briefed them on. Images of those poor, infected Indian children riddled with sores flashed through his mind while he worked on the box.

"Put your back into it!" Taylor goaded from behind his handgun and flashlight. Maddock stood stock still, watching for an opportunity. Perhaps when Bones popped the lid off, the Aussie's guard would be down sufficiently for him to make a move...

And then there was an audible *pop* as the lid came free.

Bones instinctively took a step back. "I'm suddenly thinking about smallpox."

"Hey!" Taylor warned. "Freeze! I didn't say to move!"

But he swept the pistol in Maddock's direction, wisely aware that he may be looking for an opportunity created by the slightest distraction. "You too! Freeze."

Maddock held his hands high in the air. Taylor was sounding jittery.

The aggressor spoke to Bones. "Walk over to your mate, there, while I take a look."

Bones moved to Maddock's side and stood there, stock-still.

Taylor walked over to the wheelbarrow such that he stood over the crate, facing Maddock and Bones. With the gun pointed at them, he took a look inside. Gradually his lips curved into a smile.

"I see a lot of undeveloped film." He rummaged through the box, the smile slowly disappearing. "If those are exposed, they're worth a hell of a lot, too. Could solve some mysteries once and for all, eh? But I want those stamps."

He paused, apparently mulling things over while he absentmindedly waved the gun in Maddock and Bones' direction. Still, there was about ten feet between him and them, plenty of time for him to recover if they were to make a move. They stayed put.

The Aussie apparently came to some conclusion, his gun leveling out as he began to speak once more. "All right, then. Tell you what." He glanced quickly around, then produced a small camera from his pocket. He snapped a picture of the open, film-filled crate with Maddock and Bones standing in the background. Bones blinked his eyes in the wake of the camera flash while Taylor went on.

"My little insurance policy. From here on out we're in this together, right? I've already seen the other stuff brought up so far and the stamps aren't there. So if they survived they've got to be still in the plane. If you find those stamps first, don't let anybody know. Bring them to me, and we all get a nice share. If I find 'em first, you just help me out when it comes to keeping the boss man out of the loop, and again, we all get a nice share. But I find out you're cutting me out of the action, then I make sure you have a little diving accident, and Spinney gets this photo."

He wiggled the camera in their direction. "Understood?" Maddock and Bones nodded.

"Good, now hide that crate. Don't just dump it back underwater, either, or Spinney'll know something's up. We've been over every inch of this reef and it wasn't there before. Get to it!"

Taylor waved his gun while Maddock and Bones watched the Aussie depart up the sandy path back towards camp.

CHAPTER 13

Bones shook his head, his expression one of disgust. "We really screwed that up."

Maddock moved to the crate and put the lid back on. "It could be worse. We still have the film. And at least it looks like he's keeping what he saw to himself. Hopefully we can get the other crate tomorrow and then get the heck outta here before we have to deal with him again."

Bones went to the crate and helped Maddock pat it firmly into place. "Getting access to that crate alone won't be easy. The whole team is diving on it first thing in the morning. Speaking of..." He glanced at his dive watch. "We should really get some sleep."

"Where should we hide this crate? Taking it back to camp is not an option, nor is putting it back in the water, like Taylor said."

Bones looked around the beach, up to the island's interior. "We could bury it. As long as we can remember where it is."

"Let's find a spot, up off the beach." They walked up to the edge of the water. Looking around, Maddock spotted a clump of flowering shrubs not far away.

"How about right there?"

"Let's try it." Maddock started digging while Bones brought the wheelbarrow over with the crate. They had only their dive knives to dig with, but it was sandy soil and within a few minutes they had scooped out a pit of adequate size. They slid the box in the hole, filled it back in, smoothed the surface, and covered it with vegetation so that the worked earth wasn't readily visible. They both took a look around when the job was done, making sure no one, including Taylor, was watching, though Maddock suspected that he might be.

"That'll have to do. Let's get back to camp." Maddock

went to the wheelbarrow, but then stopped short of picking it up.

"What's wrong?"

He was staring up into the island, away from the path that followed the beach in an arc to camp. "Maybe we should cut straight through there to camp, instead of following the path around."

Bones looked toward where he pointed. "Through the jungle?"

"Yeah. It's not all that thick, not like the Amazon or something like that. If we can get through it the camp is just straight across instead of all the way around, and there's less chance of somebody seeing us coming back."

"Hmmm, a little nature walk to get to my sleeping bag sooner? You make a good case, Maddock. But pushing that damn thing through the jungle?" He pointed to the wheelbarrow full of dive gear. Maddock frowned at it.

"It's pretty flat in there," he said, shining his light into the trees. "We can't just leave it here or they'll know something was going on. We need to drop it back off in the dive tent before we hit the sack."

"You push first, then."

Maddock got behind the wheelbarrow and Bones led the way into a copse of trees not far from the beach. Maddock knew that the atoll was actually comprised of several small islands very close together, and he recalled from the aerial view he had on the way in that this was not one of the thin strips of land, but the wide, triangular piece at one of the atoll's ends. At first it was easy going, with lots of space between each tree, but as they penetrated deeper into the island, the jungle truly began to live up to the name, complete with hanging vines and thick roots that they had to negotiate carefully with the wheelbarrow. It was also dark in here, the moonlight not penetrating through the canopy, so they switched on their dive lights.

Maddock checked the compass on his wrist since they were walking through a wilderness area without so much as a path. "Doesn't look like anyone from the team ever comes in here."

"It's nice and all," Bones said, stabbing his light beam into the darkness ahead, "but I can see why." All around, the hum of millions of unseen insects, birds and other animals vibrated the air, which was noticeably warmer and more humid than out on the beach. Bones slapped his arm and muttered something about mosquito repellent.

They came to an area where forward progress was no longer possible due to a pile of collapsed trees. They had to skirt around it, lifting the wheelbarrow over fallen debris as they went. When they got back on course on the other side of the tree pile, Bones pointed toward a rocky outcropping set into a small rise overgrown with vegetation. He turned his flashlight on it.

"What?" Maddock set down the wheelbarrow to look.

"Is it just me, or is there an opening in those rocks there?"

"I don't know. Does it matter?" Maddock wiped the sweat from his forehead and checked his watch. "Maybe this shortcut wasn't such a bright idea after all."

"Well, now that we're here, let me take a look." Bones walked over to the rocks. He climbed up on a couple of them and directed his light beam into the dark opening. Maddock groaned when he saw Bones waving an arm, telling him to come over.

"What for?"

"This goes back a ways. I think we should check it out."

"I thought you couldn't wait to get to sleep." Maddock reluctantly brought the wheelbarrow over to the base of the clump of boulders.

"It's a cave!"

Apparently that was all the reason Bones needed, because as Maddock watched, the big Cherokee ducked beneath an overhang of rock and disappeared into the shadowy fissure.

CHAPTER 14

"It's a full-on cave system back in here!" Bones' voice echoed back to Maddock at the entrance to the cave.

"Bones, we were in an underwater cave today, and we'll be back in it again in just a few hours. Do we really need more caves?"

"It's funny, most caves I've been in, even the more remote ones, there's always signs of human presence. Trash, something...but this one is pristine."

"Yeah, well, let's see...we're pretty much smack dab in the middle of the Pacific Ocean on a tiny, uninhabited coral atoll, and if that's not enough, we're in the most rarely visited part of *that,* in the middle of a jungle. Then you walk into a cave and wonder why no one's ever been there?"

In return Bones' light beam jiggled on the cave wall, beckoning. "C'mon! There's a fork in the road up here, I'm going left."

"Hold up, I'm on my way." Maddock didn't really want to explore the cave, but a SEAL didn't leave one of their own alone if it could be avoided. They were in this together. He followed the main tunnel straight back and down at a slight angle until he saw Bones standing at a T-intersection, playing his light on the walls. A couple of small lizards jumped past their feet and out of sight.

"I'll check the right passage, see how far it goes." Maddock had to stoop a bit to go this way, but he was able to quickly walk down the rocky corridor until it jogged to the left and opened into a smallish chamber with nothing in it. He examined the walls and ceiling with his light but found nothing of interest and headed back to where he had been with Bones.

When he got there, Bones was out of sight, so he followed the left path until it wound around to the right. Here he was faced with both a left-right fork and a higher passage that opened up in the ceiling. It was from this pathway that he heard Bones' voice emanate.

"Dude, you've got to see this! Can you hear me?"

"Sure can. Your voice is hard to miss."

"Use the foothold on the right side of the wall and jump up to the tunnel. From there it's a short walk back."

Maddock found the piece of rock and gained the tunnel . "This must have been easier for you," he said to Bones.

"Hey, my height has to be an advantage sometimes. At least you don't bang your head climbing into every freaking car ever made."

The tunnel-like area sloped down until it opened into a good-sized chamber. Bones was standing upright in the middle of it, and he had plenty of headroom. But what made this natural room special was the evidence of human presence. Maddock shone his light beam first on a small fire pit, then some piles of charred animal bones, and finally on some modern items including glass jars and plastic containers.

"So much for your *no one's ever been here before* theory." Bones grinned as he looked around the former dwelling.

Maddock walked down the short passage to join Bones in the chamber, which had obviously been occupied for some length of time in the past. "Interesting."

"What is all this crap?" Bones played his light across the objects while Maddock hunched down for a closer look.

"The bones look like fish, birds, and those might be turtles," he finished, pointing at the larger ones.

"Stuff they cooked on this fire." Bones pointed to the small ring of stones around a dirt pit still filled with ash. "So somebody camped out here for a while."

Maddock pointed at another of the objects. "And this is a glass jar, empty, possibly used for holding or collecting rain water."

"If it was water, it must have been rain water, or morning dew scraped from leaves, because this island is completely dry."

"Right. And this here," Maddock said, pointing at one

of the plastic containers without touching it, "looks like a woman's make-up holder. An old one."

"How do you know so much about make-up? Something you want to tell me?"

Maddock didn't reply. A thought had just struck him. He looked across the old fire pit at Bones, who now gaped at him. Maddock put words to both of their thoughts. "Could it be that Earhart and Noonan survived the plane crash, and lived for a time as castaways, with this being their campsite?"

Bones stroked the stubble on his chin as he pondered the notion. At length, he said, "I suppose it's possible. But make-up? Not sure why she would need make-up on the flight, though."

"I read in the briefing materials that she did a lot of media stops, like newspaper photos along the way that her husband set up. So maybe she wanted to look good."

"That's a chick for you. Speaking of pictures, we better take some." Bones removed his camera from a pocket and got some close-ups of the items without physically disturbing them.

"There's a busted knife over here." Maddock pointed to what looked like an old buck knife—a rusty blade that had become separated from its plastic handle pieces which lay nearby in the dirt. Bones photographed it.

"Hopefully Spinney doesn't see these when he appropriates our cameras to look at the dive images."

Bones laughed in agreement. "I'll take some harmless beach and dive site shots to have something in front of the wreck site images. If he scrolls back too far he'll stop there."

"Good idea. We better get back to camp."

"Did you see anything in that other passage? No human bones, I guess." The idea that Earhart had met her fate here was both creepy and exciting at the same time, and Maddock suppressed a shiver.

"Nope, nothing at all."

"Okay, let's go." They walked up the tunnel to the edge and dropped back down into the main passage. From there they retraced their steps until they reached the outer cave entrance. After climbing down the jumble of boulders and regaining flat ground, they walked back to the wheelbarrow.

"Your turn on this thing," Maddock said.

Bones shook his head. "Typical white man, adding to the red man's burden. Ro-sham-bo you for it?"

"Just take…"

Maddock's words dissolved in the thunder of a nearby explosion.

CHAPTER 15

"I think it came from the beach!" Maddock looked back the way they had come but could not see anything beyond the dense foliage.

"That'll have woken everybody up for sure. We better get over there and pretend we just got out of bed to come check it out."

"We'll have to come back for this." Maddock let go of the wheelbarrow and the two undercover SEALs ran through the jungle, the beams from their dive lights illuminating their path in chaotic, bouncy patterns.

They made rapid headway, tripping only a couple of times over exposed roots. As they neared the edge of the rain-forested area, they slowed to a walk and killed their lights. They could now see orange flames peeking through the foliage.

"Looks pretty bad." Bones started to forge his way through the last stand of trees before reaching the open area fronting the beach, but Maddock stopped him with a hand on his shoulder.

"Hold up. Hear that?"

Above the roar of the blaze they could hear people shouting.

Bones nodded. "Team's coming this way."

"We need to fall in with them so that they think we're stragglers, just waking up like they did."

"Got it." He pointed off to their left. "Let's wait over there until they pass by and then we'll fall in at the end of the line."

Maddock nodded and they crept to a copse of trees from which they could observe both the fire and the procession of people making their way toward it.

Bones pointed to the conflagration. "The pier is nothing but a fireball!"

Maddock counted the team members as they passed. "Now. Fall in. Act tired like you just got up."

"I don't have to *act* tired."

The SEAL pair slipped out of the forest without moving any branches and ambled over to the back of the line of people making their way to the pier. No one seemed to notice them sneaking out of the woods. While everyone's backs were toward them, Maddock and Bones mingled in with the group as though they had just arrived. The whole team was shouting. As they stood there in back of the group, they spotted George Taylor, who gave them a knowing smile before quickly looking away.

From this vantage point, it was clear that not only was the pier destroyed, but also the boat and seaplane. Roiling flames engulfed both. Another explosion thundered in the night as the seaplane's fuel tank detonated. The group fell to the ground, shielding their faces.

When no more explosions seemed to be forthcoming, they all got to their feet, still watching their fleet burn.

"We're stuck here now," someone pointed out.

Spinney flapped his arms like a big bird, trying to quiet everybody down so that he could say something. They did after about a minute.

"Listen up! I think we all know who's responsible for this."

War cries of "Mizuhi!" went up in unison.

"I don't see the ship," one of the divers said, scanning the water.

But then Bugsy pointed off to their left, near the edge of the lagoon. "Look! The whale!"

Maddock followed Bugsy's point in time to see a black dorsal fin slice through the water's surface in the moonlight. Spinney also looked and then turned around to address his group once more, the flaming backdrop giving his words the effect of a fiery oration.

"Mizuhi must have trained that pilot whale to stick a bomb on our pier!"

Mentally, Maddock corrected him, thinking of the

magnetic hockey-puck-sized explosive devices they had worked with in San Diego: *On the plane, since it has a metal surface.*

"Not to worry!" Spinney continued. "This is a logistical setback, but at least none of our recovered artifacts or our photographs were lost. We will get through this, people. But we need to step it up. We have to salvage as much as we can before Mizuhi does something really crazy!"

Spinney turned to his radioman. "Sims, I want you to make a report right now to all the authorities—Honolulu, the Coast Guard, Kiribati government—let everyone know what's happening here." And then, to the Australian photographer: "George! Are you getting this?" He thrust a hand toward the devastation.

Taylor held up a camera. "On it, boss." He moved away from the crowd to get unobstructed shots of the team's assets being consumed by flames. There was a hiss of steam as one of the plane's wings raised upward and it began to sink into the lagoon where the pier used to be. The Zodiac's rubber material had melted away, and the outboard was gone, probably resting on the lagoon's sandy bottom.

"This won't stop us!" Spinney reiterated. "This morning's dive is still on!"

Bugsy stepped forward. "How are we going to dive with no boat?" A chorus of *yeahs* from the team followed in the wake of the question. Spinney hesitated while looking around the island, up into the forest, and then spoke decisively.

"We'll build a raft! Let's get to work on it!"

It immediately became clear that, by *we'll* and *let's*, Spinney meant *Bugsy* and *the divers* would do the building. He quickly launched into an unnecessary set of instructions.

"Cut down some logs, gather some vines, lash them together! Get some oars! Go, go, go! If we get it done now, we can stick to our timetable. Morning dive!"

With that, Bugsy turned and rallied his troops. "You heard the man! Are we up for this! Can we do this? C'mon gents, we'll all be belly up to the Mermaid Bar in Tahiti after we get this done. And on Spinney's tab, right, boss?"

Spinney turned back around. "That's a promise!" Then he turned to the two kitchen staff and instructed them to go make some coffee. "Nobody's going back to sleep, and it's going to be a long day."

Maddock and Bones conferred rapidly in hushed tones. "Now's our chance to go get that wheelbarrow back to the dive tent." Maddock opened his eyes wide to underscore the importance of this task.

Bones nodded. "Let's tell Bugsy we're off to gather some logs for the raft."

They did so, and were sent off with enthusiastic "Attaboys!" They answered with hearty waves and headed back into the forest at approximately the same place they had emerged. As soon as the trees blocked them from view, Maddock broke into a trot.

"Come on. I doubt anyone will venture this deep inside, but we need to get to that wheelbarrow before anyone stumbles across it."

After jogging non-stop for about twenty minutes, the beams of their dive lights illuminated the rusty wheelbarrow. Bones rested with his hands on his knees for a moment, then stood.

"I still say I'll ro-sham-bo you for it."

"How about this? I'll take the wheelbarrow, but you pile those logs on top of it to cover the dive gear in case somebody sees us when we get back to camp."

Bones nodded. "Deal."

Maddock sat on a rock and rested while Bones piled the wheelbarrow with logs the proper diameter for building a raft. When he had a respectable number of logs loaded, Maddock got up and lifted the wheelbarrow.

Bones led the rest of the way through the rain forest with his light, with Maddock pushing the load. When they reached the edge of camp, they paused to see which way to the dive tent offered the least activity. Bones pointed and they sauntered into camp. On the way to the dive tent they passed right by Carlson, on his way to the research tent, who didn't even give them a second glance.

They reached the dive tent which was blessedly unoccupied, all of the divers still focused on building the raft. Maddock stood watch while Bones unloaded the logs, put the dive gear back, and then reloaded the logs onto the wheelbarrow.

He turned to Maddock. "All yours."

"No way. Your turn with it."

Bones hefted the wheelbarrow and they headed down to the beach to drop off the logs.

CHAPTER 16

A few hours later and shortly after sunrise, the entire dive team including Maddock and Bones were crowded onto a makeshift raft, paddling for the wreck site. Bruce Watanabe had insisted he come along as the "boat pilot" even though all he could do now was to help paddle and remain aboard the raft while the divers were underwater. Although the raft was slow and wet, Bones noted they actually had more room than on the Zodiac. They'd gathered many long logs and had a sizable platform on which to float.

Four of them paddling with makeshift log oars, they reached the marker in thirty minutes. Watanabe tied a line off to the buoy and then produced a pair of binoculars which he used to scan the surrounding waters for signs of Mizuhi's ship or the pilot whale. After finding nothing, he gave them the okay to dive. As Maddock slipped his mask over his head, looking around the raft at Spinney's divers, he had to admit they were dedicated to their job, and good at it. They lacked the overall stamina and of course the battle skills he and Bones possessed, but had proven they could stick with a difficult job in the face of adversity, and for that he respected them.

Bugsy gave a quick review of the dive plan, which was a repeat of the previous day's dive. Four divers were to penetrate the plane and recover artifacts from it, including Maddock and Bones, while the other two were to explore the tunnel system for human remains. On shore there had been a tense moment when Bugsy had assigned Maddock and Bones to the tunnel team, which would have prevented them access to the plane. But Maddock had talked him into letting he and Bones be part of the airplane team again because they had seen something yesterday they wanted to follow up on—a specific place within the aircraft that would be difficult for someone else to find. Bugsy had shrugged and asked the other divers if they had any objections. The two who had been inside the plane yesterday said they wouldn't mind giving the tunnels a try this time, and so it was settled.

Now, the six of them rolled off the raft into the ocean and followed the buoy line down to the edge of the reef. They spread out in a horizontal line and dropped down the wall to the ledge. There, Maddock and Bones again made a beeline for the tunnel, since once inside it was single file without sufficient room to pass anyone, guaranteeing them to be first to arrive at the plane.

Maddock led the way down the left passage toward the plane, the other three wreck divers behind him, including Bones, while the two tunnel explorers moved off along the right-side passage. Upon reaching the Electra chamber, Maddock swam directly through the windshield without slowing. Bones was close behind.

"You guys have that maneuver down," the diver next in line noted.

"Practice makes perfect." Maddock swam through the airplane to the furl of sheet metal covering the remaining crate. He looked into Bones' eyes while he spoke, to emphasize the importance of the communication that everyone would be able to hear.

"*Keith*, I'm going to unroll this metal here. This is what I noticed yesterday. You check the extreme rear cargo area for anything we might not have seen."

"Copy that," Bones said. "You can extract the box from the aluminum coils by himself, so I may as well have a look around and see if I can find anything else that might relate to the mission. After all, this is hopefully our last dive."

The other two divers entered the cockpit and began to scour the forward cargo section and cockpit areas.

Maddock had removed most of the aircraft metal off the top of the crate when he sliced his hand on the thin metal sheet like a paper cut, right through the glove, resulting in a drifting cloud of blood that looked black unless he shone his light directly on it. He cursed softly but one of the other divers still asked him what happened. He saw no reason to suppress the truth at this point and told them he cut his hand on some metal while removing an "object of interest."

"What is it?" one of them asked.

"Looks like a box. I've almost got it free."

Bones swam over to see how it was going, since it would probably seem strange not to. He helped Maddock pull the box out from under the last of the metal and they examined its seal. It looked good and tight, though they didn't want to call attention to that fact. Maddock eyed Spinney's two divers up front, both of them busy searching nooks and crannies. He mouthed the words, "Find anything?" to Bones, who shook his head.

Remembering how difficult it was to get the other crate to the surface, Maddock pointed to the crate and then up. Bones nodded. If anything, Maddock thought, this box was heavier than the first one. They might as well get a move on, even if they had to wait for the rest of the team for a bit on the raft. There was nothing else here for them besides this crate.

Maddock notified the other divers that the box was heavy and that he and "Keith" had best get started wrangling it out of the plane, through the tunnel and rigging the lift bag for the trip to the surface. They agreed, saying they'd either meet them on the ledge or else see them at the decompression stop.

Maddock and Bones worked together to move the box to the plane's cockpit. They took extra care not to jostle it too much, knowing what it might contain. One of the other divers helped them shove it through the windshield and swim it up to the tunnel entrance. Then he went back to the airplane and Maddock and Bones were on their own to get the box to the boat. Maddock briefly entertained the notion of dumping the box on the reef again for later pickup and saying they dropped it over the ledge into the deep, but decided against it. Paddling back out here at night in the raft wasn't an attractive option, and he felt a kind of Spidey-sense telling him that it would be pushing their already maxed-out luck.

When they reached the mouth of the tunnel, overlooking the ledge where the Electra's tail protruded from the cave, Maddock was tempted to simply slide the box over the edge, letting it tumble through the water to the bottom below. However, on the off chance that this thing really did contain some kind of smallpox bombs, he decided that they better do it the hard way. He and Bones each held onto the crate and swam it down gently to the bottom in an upright position. From there, they lugged it to the edge of the wall, where thousands of feet of ocean lay below them, and two hundred feet beckoned above.

Bones deployed the lift bag and they rigged it to the crate. When it was ready, Maddock said into the comm system, "Okay, we're leaving from the ledge with the—"

He interrupted his communication as a flash of black entered his peripheral vision.

"Say again—you're breaking up," one of the tunnel divers said, not realizing Maddock had simply stopped speaking. It was Bones who responded.

"We've got a whale of a problem out here!"

CHAPTER 17

The pilot whale homed in on them. As it neared the ledge, however, Maddock could see that something was different about it. "Shankey's not living up to his name." He focused on the animal's rostrum, where the blade had been attached.

"You're right," Bones said, "I don't see a bayonet on it anymore. But I do see something..."

Maddock stared at the object the whale carried in some kind of harness. He was struggling to make it out when he saw the blinking LED light.

"*Bomb,* incoming!" With respect to his cover, the military jargon wasn't the best choice of words, but right now that was the least of his concerns. Three tons of trained whale was driving right at them strapped with an armed explosive device, two-hundred feet underwater.

Maddock glanced backward, confirming his suspicions. They stood directly between the whale and the airplane, its metal surface no doubt the whale's intended target for its hockey-puck-sized payload.

"I'm fresh out of lobsters, got any ideas?" Despite the attempt at humor, the tension in Maddock's voice was palpable as the whale neared. He looked over at Bones and saw him fiddling with one of his gear hoses.

"Keith, what's up, it's almost on us!" He didn't see how they were going to stop the massive animal from going where it wanted to go.

Then he heard a sound sort of like a car horn. Loud, disconcerting. Underwater, it was difficult to pinpoint the direction from where a sound originated, but when he looked over at Bones he saw him holding his mouthpiece in one hand and blowing into some sort of contraption attached to his buoyancy compensator hose. Maddock felt a sense of hope as he realized what it was. An underwater signal horn, it was a noisemaker used to attract the attention of nearby divers. But in this case, he supposed Bones was hoping it would annoy the hell out of this whale and distract it from planting the bomb on the airplane.

As the cetacean came in on a trajectory that would take it directly over their heads and right to the Electra, it suddenly sheared off to the left, arcing away from them as it swam nearly upside-down. Bones continued to blast away on the horn while Maddock added to the cacophony by rapping on the back of his scuba tank with his dive knife, hoping the piercing underwater signature would disorient the beast.

Maddock watched as the whale circled tightly and came at them again. This time, however, its course was lower and skewed more to the left of the airplane. It barreled in fast, causing Maddock and Bones to move closer to the edge, Bones dragging the crate and its lift bag with him. Then, as the pilot whale reached the ledge to their right, it belly-scraped as it rode up onto the rocky shelf.

The other divers were calling out, now, "What's going on? What's happening?"

"Whale's trying to stick a bomb on the plane," Maddock blurted out in a rush of words.

They watched as the big animal spasmodically twisted around after hitting the coral shelf, closer than before to the sound of Bones' incessant horn blowing. It writhed in place before swimming off into open water without having come into contact with the aircraft.

Yet, as Maddock examined the patch of coral where a cloud of sediment now began to settle, he saw that it had left something behind. A small, disc-shaped object.

The bomb.

It had probably dislodged accidentally when the whale scraped its belly against the ledge, but it didn't matter why it was there. It was there, and judging by the LED's hectic blinking, it had been activated.

Maddock quickly calculated the distance between himself and the explosive device. It was set way back on the ledge, almost to the coral wall the plane disappeared into.

Don't.

He had considered swimming to it, picking it up, and returning to the ledge to drop it over the side in hopes it would explode down along the wall. But the little voice in his head told him there wasn't enough time. He grabbed Bones by the arm and pointed to the surface.

"Let's go!"

He then warned the other divers. "Bugsy—you guys back there—brace yourselves, bomb's gonna blow!"

Bones put some more air into the lift bag so that it would rise faster and then he and Maddock kicked off from the ledge toward the surface. They had just cleared the overhang when the bomb went off.

Underwater, the sound was muted to a dull rumble, but they felt the pressure waves in the water, even separated from the blast by the coral overhang. Maddock knew from their Basic Underwater Demolition School training that had that rocky buffer not been between them and the explosion, they almost certainly would have been killed. As it was, he felt a sharp pain in his ears. He and Bones looked at one another. The stout Indian indicated he was fine, and still clutched the lift bag with the crate.

Then, just as they resumed their ascent, the coral overhang crumbled and broke away from the wall beneath them. Maddock and Bones hovered in place, trying to see through the cloud of debris created by the falling overhang. When it did clear, they had trouble believing their eyes.

Maddock was the first to voice his concern over what they saw. "Bugsy, get everybody outta there! The whole ledge is crumbling!"

No sooner had he finished his sentence than they watched in astounded horror as the coral shelf broke away and slid into the deep...

...and with it, Amelia Earhart's famed Electra.

Maddock and Bones watched dumbfounded as the legendary aircraft nosedived into the depths with the falling coral, as if on a final flight into the abyss.

As captivating as the sight was, Maddock could think of only one thing. He yelled into his mask mic.

"Bugsy? What's your status?" The comm channel filled with blaring static. Maddock looked at Bones. He was about to tell him to surface with the crate alone while he went back down to make sure the other divers were okay when he saw the two men who had been in the plane swimming up toward them from where the ledge used to be.

Then Bugsy's voice came over the comm line, frantic, frayed, stunned.

"I'm out! I'm out! But Scotty...he's still in there! Tunnel collapsed!"

Bones pointed to his air pressure gauge. It was in the red. Maddock's was too.

"Is there anything we can do for him?" Maddock returned.

"Negative. *Negative*! He's already...he's dead, crushed, I *saw* it!" Bugsy's voice cracked while he swam. "It's still coming down." Then, after a short pause: "My God—what happened to the ledge? Where's the *plane*? Where am I?"

Maddock began to swim for the surface while he responded, helping Bones drag the lift-bag. "It all went over the edge, Bugsy."

"Everybody to the reef for decompression, that's an order!"

"Copy that." Maddock and Bones led the way to the shallow reef where they used nearly all of their remaining air supply to decompress. They were joined by Bugsy and the two other surviving divers. They sat in a circle formation facing outward in case the pilot whale decided to return, but a few minutes later when they were ready to swim up to the raft, it had still not shown itself. Maddock wondered aloud if it could have been knocked unconscious in the blast and drowned, sinking into the depths along with Earhart's plane. Everyone said they hoped so.

Amazingly, Maddock noticed, each of the two divers who had been in the airplane with them still carried bags of artifacts they'd collected.

At the raft, Watanabe helped Maddock and Bones gingerly load the crate onto the improvised transport. They repeatedly insisted that he be extremely careful with it. After all they'd been through, the very last thing they needed was to give everyone smallpox by knocking the crate around too hard and releasing the virus, if it was there. They told Watanabe they were highly concerned about whatever artifacts were inside since they now represented the last of whatever they would be able to recover. The boat pilot thanked them for their careful work.

The row back to shore was somber, the men not talking, with the exception of Watanabe, who had the unenviable job of reporting the events of the dive to Spinney. The expedition leader was there on the beach with Carlson and Taylor when the raft arrived, its crew exhausted, shaken and solemn. Taylor snapped off multiple pictures of the returning raft and the divers. Spinney was already calling out to the team before any of them had stepped ashore, asking if the airplane was okay.

No one was in the mood to respond.

CHAPTER 18

Spinney's face went beet red the moment he heard about the airplane sliding into the abyss. He'd already issued his grandiose press release to media outlets around the world, and in an effort to save face, he made Watanabe repeat himself four times. He even went so far as to question each diver independently as to what they saw, which naturally did nothing to change the outcome. Amelia Earhart's plane was gone once again, and with it Spinney's dreams. Perhaps it was still gliding to the bottom of the ocean as they spoke, but regardless, it would end up well beyond the range of any salvage technology Spinney had access to.

He stomped around the beach, pacing like a caged tiger, imploring his men as they prepared to haul their gear back to camp for the last time.

"We still found it!" Spinney bellowed after them. "It's not like we don't have proof. We know where it is!"

No one answered him.

"What about the artifacts from this dive? I see the crate." He pointed to the box Maddock and Bones had just set down in the soft sand. "Anything else?"

The two divers who had been inside the plane with Maddock and Bones stepped forward and wordlessly handed Spinney their bags containing the odds and ends they had recovered from Earhart's plane.

"Steve, let's get a workup going on this new stuff and see what we have. We'll also have to send a follow-up on the press release..."

"We just lost a man..."

"He's gone. Nothing we can do about it." Spinney continued blathering on about his next steps as the team began trooping back to camp in a single file line along the beach path. One of the divers pushed the wheelbarrow filled with dive gear. Spinney and Carlson led the way up front, while Maddock and Bones brought up the rear with the new crate. They had improvised a simple carry rig for it out of two tree branches left over from the raft construction. They set the old crate in the middle of the two branches, spaced about two feet apart, and then each picked up one end, with Bones leading. George Taylor walked alongside them for a stretch, snapping pictures of them carrying the box while giving them a wink in between shots before falling back in line ahead of them.

Maddock's mind was spinning as Spinney chattered on up ahead about research plans and media kits and television appearances....What would they do if the crate they now carried was opened and it contained something of value to their military objectives? For Spinney's team just to *see* something like that, even if Maddock and Bones appropriated the items afterward, would be less than optimal with regard to their mission. And no doubt, after the press conference, the explosion, and now *this,* the little atoll was about to be overrun with authorities. He knew Bones was aware that today was the day they had to make their escape, but he had no idea how soon their opportunity would arise.

Maddock was jarred from his strategic thoughts by a sharp rise in the volume of conversation by the team members walking ahead of them. Bugsy was yelling at the back of Spinney's head.

"Don, maybe you haven't noticed, but Scotty's *dead*! He's not ever coming back from that tunnel down there! I know you're upset about the airplane, but couldn't you show the least bit of sympathy?"

Spinney said something in a lower voice Maddock couldn't distinguish.

"What's that, you bastard?" Bugsy stepped out of the line and walked around Carlson, butting up to Spinney.

"Say it again. I said say it *again*, old man!"

Apparently Spinney repeated whatever it was he had said, because the next thing everybody knew, Bugsy swung a roundhouse right to his jaw and Spinney stumbled backward over a tree root, Bugsy jumping on top of him.

The divers, Taylor, and Carlson all crowded around the two grappling men, shouting for them to stop. Maddock quickly scanned their surroundings while he and Bones stood frozen in place, each holding one end of the poles with the crate balanced in the middle. They were at the foot of the jungle trail that led into the overgrown heart of the island. Neither Spinney nor Bugsy had responded to the shouted requests to knock it off, so the divers now got down and tousled with them, attempting to separate the two fighting men.

Maddock raised his eyebrows at Bones and cocked his head toward the trail head. Bones glanced that way and nodded. Then the two of them silently moved off onto the new path, rounded a clump of foliage and moved as quickly as they dared into the jungle.

They had gone about twenty feet when Maddock tripped over a protruding knob of coral and he went sprawling, dropping his end of the sticks. With Bones holding up his end only, the box slid down the branch rails until it hit the ground and tipped over. The large Cherokee's eyes grew wide as saucers as he stared at the upended crate.

Maddock gently righted the container and they reloaded it onto the supports. They quickly got moving again.

"Where to?" Bones wanted to know.

"To the cave!"

A few seconds after that they heard their cover names being called from over on the beach path. Their absence, and no doubt that of the crate, had been noticed.

They increased their awkward gait as they moved into the jungle proper after the footpath ended. Maddock asked Bones to stop and set the poles down so he could consult his compass. He took a bearing and then they headed off toward the cave entrance.

When they reached it they set the crate down at the foot of the opening in the jumble of rocks. They couldn't hear any signs of a pursuit, but knew it wouldn't be long. After all, with the boat and the seaplane destroyed, there was nowhere they could have gone.

"It's going to be a bitch getting this thing up there." Bones breathed heavily while he looked up at the opening into the cave system. Scrambling up the haphazard array of boulders while not carrying anything was easy enough, but with a weighty box possibly containing a deadly bio-weapon, the task became anything but simple. Nevertheless, they needed a hiding place, and a good one.

"We've probably got a thirty-minute grace period from now while they think we just went somewhere else to avoid the confrontation of the fight," Maddock hypothesized.

"But after that they'll turn this little patch of coral upside down looking for us."

"Let's get a move on."

They spent a couple of precious minutes eyeballing the best route for them to take up to the cave—handholds, footholds, resting points. They decided not to use the poles and hid them in the brush. They also took care to disguise any trampled vegetation or other signs of their passage.

That done, they both put their hands on the crate and began to take it up the rocky incline. Fifteen minutes later, they slid the mysterious box up into the cave. They looked down over the jungle, double-checking for anything that would give away their presence to someone who passed through here searching for them. Satisfied they had left behind no obvious signs, Maddock and Bones turned their attention back to the crate and the cave.

Bones gauged the distance to the back wall where passages went left and right. "Not really looking forward to lugging this thing all the way to the room back there," he said, referencing the chamber filled with evidence of human activity.

"Let's open it here and see what's in it. That way we can keep an eye on what's happening out there." He looked out over the jungle.

Bones nodded. "Plus if it doesn't have anything that has to do with our mission we can just get rid of it." He unsheathed his dive knife while Maddock provided extra illumination with his flashlight. After crushing off the marine growth, Bones was able to pry up the lid. Maddock lifted it off the container and they looked inside.

Maddock and Bones remained quiet as they stared into the crate. They were looking at a plastic tray of off-white, ceramic spheres. Each bore a black skull-and-crossbones label. A second tray of the same was visible underneath the top layer.

"Rows of four by four, so sixteen on top, sixteen on bottom for thirty-two total," Maddock calculated.

"I'm just looking to see if any are cracked." Bones stared intently into the box.

"It doesn't look like any of these top ones are. We should check the ones underneath, though."

Bones exhaled heavily. "Why the skull-and-crossbones and not the biohazard symbol?"

"I don't think that was in use until later."

"So how are we going to do this?" Bones eyed the crate's contents dubiously.

Maddock ran a finger lightly over one of the trays. "I think the supports are plastic, so I don't think we need to worry about them crumbling if we lift it out."

"They had plastic in 1937?"

"Yeah. I don't think they had so many different kinds like they do now, but they had it."

"Are you sure? Because if this stuff turns to dust and one of those ceramic things breaks..."

Maddock lightly traced a finger along the framework in which the bio-weapons were nestled.

"It's plastic, Bones. C'mon, we've either been infected already or we haven't. Let's lift out this top tray and find out." Maddock balanced his dive light on a shelf of rock so that it shone on the box, freeing both hands.

"At least we had the vaccine. Remind me to get that nurse's number when we go back for the debriefing..."

"Bones. Stay on track. The whole island is looking for us and we still have a lot to do."

"Okay. You're not about to have any kind of muscle spasm or anything, right?" Bones flexed his fingers as

Maddock felt around the tray for a place from which to lift it.

"I'll be okay. How about if I lift it out with two hands, and you cup your hands underneath to catch one of these globes in case it falls through."

"Where are you going to set the tray down after you lift it out?"

Maddock looked at the ground next to them and pointed. "Right there."

Bones used his knife to rake the spot clean and even, making sure there were no rocks just beneath the dirt waiting to crack the ceramic spheres.

Maddock gripped the tray and began to lift.

CHAPTER 19

"Seems sturdy." Maddock tested the tray by raising it by only a millimeter and holding it there. He lifted it a little higher, the plastic retaining its integrity. "Here goes." Maddock held the tray full of ceramic spheres high enough for Bones to hold his big hands beneath it as a safety net.

After a few seconds, he told Bones to look underneath. "We need to make sure the bottoms are intact." Maddock held the tray of smallpox bombs steady while Bones moved his head beneath it and aimed his light on the undersides of the ceramic vessels.

"Looks like they're all in one piece. I don't see any hairline fractures or anything."

Maddock set the tray down gently on the dirt floor of the cave and then directed his light beam on the second tray at the bottom of the crate. Bones peered in at them.

"They look good from this angle."

"We've got to get a look at the bottoms of these, too." They repeated the process with this tray, Bones eyeing the lower surface of the containers.

"No cracks, no holes! We're smallpox free!"

Maddock eased the tray back into the bottom of the crate. Then he and Bones carefully put the first tray back on top of that one and put the lid back on the crate, making sure it was fastened securely. He looked at the sealed crate and shook his head, amazed that his government had enlisted the famous aviatrix to drop these horrendous viral bombs on other human beings.

"What I don't get," Maddock said, standing and looking out once again over the jungle, "is why her plane was full of bullet holes when it crashed over what at the time was U.S-held territory. The Japanese were hundreds of miles further north in the Marshalls."

Bones looked at the crate while he thought. "Maybe she

went through there and that's where she took the hits, but made it back down this way as far as she could until the damage took its toll and she crashed."

"I find it hard to believe that she would have made it hundreds of miles if the damage was that significant. That plane was shot up pretty bad, with a lot of the rounds going right into the fuel tanks. Also, there's something else that bothers me."

"You've got no game with the ladies?"

Maddock rolled his eyes. "The Japanese didn't use that caliber of rounds. I measured one of the bullet holes in the side of the plane using the ruler marks that are etched into my knife blade. They're definitely 50 millimeters. Not a caliber the Japanese were using at that time."

"So what are you saying?"

At that moment they heard a steady rushing sound as it began to rain hard outside the cave. They viewed it as a positive thing, since it would make searching for them more difficult, and the water would wash away any of their tracks they may have failed to conceal.

"I'm saying..." Maddock seemed to have trouble formulating what he was about to put forth. "What if she was shot down by our own guys?"

"Friendly fire?"

Maddock shrugged. "I'm thinking not so friendly fire. Jimmy said that some rumors have it that Earhart was captured by the Japanese. If her plane went down in the Marshalls and they found her with these..." He looked at the crate. Bones' eyes widened.

"You think they would have sent her back down this way to deliver the smallpox to the American forces?"

"Exactly! Or even just to take pictures with those dome cameras and bring them back to the Japanese. And if they did, the U.S. Navy, knowing what weapons she had at her disposal," again he nodded at the crate, "might have ordered her shot down in order to save more lives."

Bones stared out at the falling rain. "Amelia Earhart shot down by the U.S. Navy as a counterspy? If the

American public knew about that..."

Maddock shook his head. "It's our job to make sure they never know unless the government wants them to know, Bones. We just need to get this thing back to the Navy that's all."

Bones nodded. "This thing and the other crate, too. Speaking of..."

Maddock frowned as he stared out into the beating rain. "We have to go dig up the first crate with the film and bring it back here. Then we can make our extraction call."

Bones grinned in agreement. "So let's get that other crate."

"Agreed. Either we go now under cover of this rain, or we wait until nightfall, what do you think?"

In response, Bones laced his shoes down tight. "Let's get it done."

After surveying the immediate area outside the cave to be certain no one was there, the pair of SEALs made their way down to the jungle floor.

CHAPTER 20

If anything, the rain seemed to be intensifying. The jungle floor had been transformed into a muddy bog that slowed their forward progress considerably. The forest canopy kept the brunt of the rain's force off of their heads, but there was still a constant trickle and the sound of water bombarding the leaves overhead was almost deafening.

Making matters worse, Maddock and Bones had to stick to the most concealed areas—dense brambles of underbrush, hopelessly entwined thickets of vines and branches—lest they come into view of a search party caught in the rain. They figured that Spinney's team would be safe in their tents by now, but as SEALs they trained and prepared for the unexpected. Whenever possible, they would always opt for the safest route that would still get the job done, not the easiest.

The going was slow but they kept on, and in a couple of hours Maddock stiff-armed Bones' back as he crouched behind the last thick tree before the jungle gave way to the flat, grassy area that led to the beach. The buried crate lay just up ahead.

"Let's watch." Maddock and Bones monitored the area for several minutes, the rain still sheeting down around them.

"Good thing we're here to get this thing," Bones whispered. "This rain's going to wash away the dirt over the crate in no time, if it hasn't already."

Maddock agreed. The thin cover of sandy soil they'd hurriedly heaped on top of the box couldn't possibly withstand this kind of deluge for long. He put his index and middle fingers together and pointed toward the cluster of flowering bushes where they'd buried the film crate.

He and Bones moved out from behind the tree cover and ran to the site of the buried strongbox. The gray sky and the rain coming down hard made them question at first if they were at the same landmark clump of vegetation, but they found the hole they dug on the side closest to the beach.

Unfortunately, that's what it was: a hole.

"Dude! Someone stole our crate!" Bones stared into the empty pit, now filling with sandy mud. Maddock looked around in case someone was still nearby, but he saw no one. He walked slowly around the area, thoroughly checking the ground to see if any clues had been left behind, or if by chance the crate had simply been washed away to a nearby spot. There was nothing.

"It must be George Taylor." Maddock kicked the tip of his shoe into the wet ground in frustration.

Bones nodded slowly, the reality hitting him hard. "When we split with the smallpox crate, Taylor probably figured we were trying to rip him off and so he went back and took this one in retaliation." He pointed at the empty gap in the earth.

"And he probably thinks the crate we took off with is loaded with those cancelled stamps. If he only knew..." Maddock laughed hollowly.

"We've got to get that film back. It's the other half of our objective."

"Right. So the question is, did Taylor hide the film somewhere else for himself, or did he share that we buried it with the team, to label us as thieves and traitors?"

Bones shook his head slowly. "Not good. If he buried it somewhere else..."

"Hopefully he's got it just sitting in his tent." Maddock's suggestion was a spark of hope, because sneaking into Taylor's tent and taking the film back was something they could do. Unfortunately, so was kidnapping Taylor and torturing the location of the film out of him. They definitely did not want to do anything like that, but it was something that would be well within their duty as SEALs to do, should there be absolutely no other alternative. Poor Taylor thought that he was dealing with a couple of random commercial divers out to make a few extra bucks on a job. It was their job to be underestimated like that, though, and they didn't hold it against him.

Bones held up a finger. "The other possibility, if he turned it over to Spinney, is that the whole team could now be guarding it along with the other artifacts."

That would also present a serious problem. The two of them could easily deal with Taylor, but the whole team at once? Even SEALs had their limits. Neither Maddock nor Bones had a firearm with him, but they already knew that Taylor did. And they suspected Spinney probably did, too, although they didn't know for certain.

"I know one thing," Maddock said, standing and facing toward the beach path that led to camp. "Late tomorrow people will start arriving here to investigate Spinney's Mizuhi accusations and sensational press releases. We need to be gone by then. I don't think waiting until tonight to sneak into camp is a good idea."

"They'll probably be expecting us to do that, anyway, and have guards posted. Or if it's only Taylor in on this, you know he'll be sleeping with one eye open."

"Daytime surprise attack?"

"It's on like Donkey Kong. Jungle shortcut again?"

Maddock agreed and they retreated into the jungle.

"Let's just hope," Maddock says, "that the attack really does turn out to be a surprise."

CHAPTER 21

Maddock and Bones concealed themselves in some tall weeds just outside of camp. They could hear electronic chatter coming from the radio tent, but other than that saw no signs of activity. The rain had let up a little but was still coming down. They moved off in a crouching run toward the sleeping tents.

When they neared them, they were mortified to see George Taylor himself walk into his tent, coming from the campfire area. Bones muttered a curse under his breath. He looked at Maddock. *Now what?*

Bones pointed at Taylor's tent. They would have to do what they would have to do. Just as they were about to move, Taylor exited his tent, walking back the way he had come. Maddock exhaled as he and Bones crouched low to the ground. They waited until Taylor had walked out of sight, and then sprang into action.

They sprinted to the tent and ducked inside. There was a sleeping bag on the floor, a packing crate—not an artifact—used as a small table on which sat a lantern and a camera, and a stack of books about Amelia Earhart on a covered table of some sort.

Maddock indicated with hand signals for Bones to keep watch. The big Indian crouched behind the tent flap, peeking outside while Maddock slid the books to the floor and uncovered the table.

The crate!

But would it still contain the film?

He hissed at Bones. "Crate's here, I'm going to open it. Stay on post."

Bones continued to keep watch while Maddock used his dive knife to pry open the crate. There was only the sound of rain pattering on the tent fabric while he evaluated what lay inside.

The same undeveloped film rolls they'd seen before.

"It's here!" He removed his backpack and opened it, setting it on the floor next to the crate. "I'm going to put the film in my pack so we don't have to carry the damn crate, and Taylor might not know for a while the film's been taken from it."

"Good idea." Bones' head turned back and forth as he maintained watch.

Maddock found a small knapsack and a large Ziploc bag, and packed up all the film. He put the pack on his back. Then he put the lid back on the crate, covered it with the blanket again, and finally put the books back on top as they were before.

"Let's go!"

"Hold on! Someone's coming!"

Bones pointed to the right from the open tent door. Two of the divers walked toward them, talking in hushed tones. Maddock and Bones shrunk back from the tent door. The divers continued walking past Taylor's tent and ducked inside the tent next to it.

Breathing a heavy sigh of relief, Maddock pointed through the tent's far wall to the jungle. Bones nodded, and the two SEALs ran from the tent to the nearest cover of foliage. From there they low-crawled to the edge of the jungle, where they listened for signs of people. Hearing none, they stood and crept into the forest.

The trip through the jungle was again slow and arduous, with much rainwater accumulated on the ground. They continued to be stealthy, not assuming that no one would be looking for them in here. Covered in mud, they painted their faces to further camouflage themselves. An hour later they neared the cave.

After crouching in the leaves of a fallen tree for a few minutes to ascertain it was safe to proceed, Maddock and Bones ran to the bottom of the boulder jumble that led up to the mouth of their hiding place. They climbed up inside it. Maddock shrugged off the backpack and set it down next to the crate containing the smallpox.

Maddock gave Bones a high-five. "We've got everything we need to make the Commander happy."

"Now if we can just get off this godforsaken rock."

Maddock pulled open his backpack to pull out the satellite phone. "Let's make that extraction call. They said it would be—"

Maddock cut himself short, a hand still groping around inside the pack.

"What is it?" Bones eyed the pack with alarm.

"It's..." Maddock trailed off once again as if unwilling to commit to a statement that scared him.

"It's gone? Tell me it's not freaking gone, Maddock!"

Maddock held the pack upside down and shook it. He unzipped a few of the larger side pockets and searched inside. He shook his head.

"I could tell you it's not gone, but I'd be lying." He looked up from the pack to Bones, whose mouth dropped open in stunned disbelief. He glanced around the cave, in case it might be lying in view on the ground somewhere. But besides his own small pack and the crate, there was only the moist, smooth packed dirt of the cave floor.

"Hold on..." Bones took off his own small pack and rifled through it. He threw it back down. He eyeballed the box. "No possible way it could have fallen in with the smallpox?"

"Nope."

"Maybe it was in the film crate and we didn't notice it in Taylor's tent?"

"I think you're on the right track with Taylor, or somebody from Spinney's team, but I looked in there with a flashlight, Bones, and it wasn't in there."

"Okay." He looked over at Maddock, who was once again checking his pack. "So what could have happened to it? When's the last time you saw it for sure? The last time I saw it was when you used it to call Jimmy."

Maddock gazed at the cave ceiling while he thought. "Last time I know I saw it was on the raft right before the dive."

"You brought the sat-phone with you on the raft?"

"Yeah. I took it out on all the dives and left it on the boat, including the raft."

"What the heck for?"

Maddock shrugged. "For one thing, who knows, maybe we might need it..." Bones frowned and Maddock continued. "For another, I didn't like the idea of just leaving it in our tent all day for Spinney and Carlson to snoop and find while we were out diving."

Bones gave an accepting expression. "I can see that. So you think Bruce Watanabe could have snagged it from your pack while we were under?"

"It's possible. He seems like a nice guy, but..."

"He's loyal to Spinney and Spinney's kind of a douche."

"True, but it also could have been anyone else. Bugsy? The radio guy, what's his name?"

"Harvey."

Maddock nodded. "Harvey Sims, that's it."

"He was never around the campfire much when we were, either," Bones added.

"And let's not forget about the fearless leader himself."

"Yeah, Spinney wasn't around the fire much, either."

Maddock stood up and began to pace the confines of the narrow cave, staring out at the dark jungle when he reached the mouth and then at Bones on the way back. "Okay let's think about the situation. We're ready for extraction but have no way to contact the extraction team or our handlers, at least without blowing our cover."

Bones nodded, assuming a mocking tone. "Excuse me, Mr. Spinney, do you have a satellite phone we can use, because we need to call the Navy to tell them to pick us up in one of those black helicopters because they want the stuff we took from Amelia Earhart's plane as soon possible. He'll understand, right?"

Maddock thought for a moment. "Getting serious for a second, I think it's safe to say that Spinney probably sleeps with his sat-phone…"

"Up his tailpipe," Bones cut in.

Maddock grimaced. "We can also assume we wouldn't be able to get it without starting a major confrontation."

Bones gave a gesture of non-commitment. "I'm ready."

"If it comes to that, then we have no choice, but there might be a clandestine option left."

"Do tell."

"We just mentioned Sims."

"Yeah, Harvey and all his geek toys in that tent full of…oh!" Bones' face lit with awareness.

"Yeah. The ham radio tent. We could use the shortwave set to send Morse to Base Team."

"It might be overheard."

"By a few random radio operators around the world, sure, but the frequency is pretty obscure. The biggest worry is just being seen physically in the radio tent by anyone."

"Do you know the frequency they would use? Because I forgot that along with most of that academic crap they tested us on once upon a time."

Maddock thought for a moment. "I'm pretty sure I do. And worse comes to worse we could ask an amateur radio operator to relay a coded verbal message."

"So how do we get at that radio gear? Sims is always in there. He'll be in there now for sure with everything going on with the press releases and whatnot."

"Except when he's sleeping. So we wait until the middle of the night."

Bones looked out at the rainy jungle. "Great! All we have to do is sit around for about eight hours, right?"

"Six ought to do, including travel time."

Bones nodded. "Sounds good to me. We stay out of trouble and get some shuteye in here for the next five hours."

Maddock lay down on his back on the tunnel floor. "How about I get some shut-eye for the first two-and-a-half while you keep watch, then you sleep two-and-a-half while I watch. After that it'll be time to move."

Bones nodded and moved a little closer to the edge of the cave. "Sweet dreams, Maddock. Go easy on the snoring."

Maddock glanced at his watch just before he closed his eyes. If all went well they'd be making their extraction call tonight.

CHAPTER 22

"Rise and shine, Sleeping Beauty." Maddock gave the snoring Bones a shove, both of them having slept their respective shifts. The startled Indian raised a fist, which Maddock clamped in a steady hand.

"Save it for anyone who gets in our way. It's go-time."

Maddock shouldered his backpack and stared outside the cave at the jungle. The rain had stopped, leaving only the sounds of millions of insects, blended with a few birdcalls and the dripping of water onto the forest floor.

Maddock took out his camera and scrolled through its pictures until he found the aerial shots he'd taken from the helicopter on the way in. He showed one to Bones. "So this is what I was thinking. You see the radio tent there..." The large tent and the antenna tower were clearly visible in the shot.

"I see it."

Maddock passed a fingernail over the tiny screen. "Over here is a thick stand of plants, and then the lagoon beach past that."

"You want to hang out in those bushes while we scout out the tent?"

"I don't really *want* to, Bones, as much I enjoy your company, but I think it offers the best chance of not being seen until we establish what's happening in and around the radio tent."

"What's the best way to get there?"

Maddock studied the aerial image and traced a finger across the small screen while he spoke. "We go through the jungle like we're taking a shotcut to camp, but before we get to the end, we cut through here." He jabbed his finger at a spot on the display. "We'll come out on this narrow strip of lagoon beach, with the jungle still shielding us from the camp side."

Bones dragged his meaty finger across the camera. "Then we just walk along the beach to that clump of bushes you were talking about to scope out the tent."

"That's it. Ready?"

"Sure could use a strong cup of coffee," Bones said, stretching in the mouth of the cave.

"Wrestling this box full of smallpox down those rocks should be a good wake-up call."

Maddock hefted the crate and walked over to Bones, who took half its weight. Together they eased the old box down the rocky incline until they reached the soggy ground. Maddock retrieved the poles they used to carry the box, placed the box on the poles as before, switched their dive lights on, and began to move once again through the rain forest.

The going was slow in the darkness over the waterlogged ground, and they had no desire to push their luck knowing what was inside the crate should they drop it. They plodded onward, glancing now and then at their watches, dreading the possibility of finding Sims already at work in the radio tent when they got there. He was known to keep odd hours in order to best utilize atmospheric phenomena that might offer the best radio wave propagation. The crate felt heavier than ever and they had to stop and rest every so often.

After what seemed like a long while they recognized a grouping of trees and knew that they were almost to the end of the jungle where it opened onto the path leading to camp.

"We cut through there." Maddock pointed through what looked like the thickest possible part of the jungle. He knew from the aerial photograph that the atoll's lagoon lay not far on the other side of it. They set off into it, moving slower than before and stopping frequently to set the poles down while they used their knives to cut vines out of the way or chop down obstructing branches.

After an exhausting trek they cautiously emerged onto the narrow ribbon of sand fronting the lagoon. After listening and watching they saw no reason not to continue and took up the poles again. They walked along the sand, welcoming the warm breeze wafting off the lagoon. When they reached the cluster of foliage Maddock had picked out in the aerial photo, they briefly surveyed the area. Quiet all around.

They dragged the crate deep inside the plants and hid the poles. They situated themselves so that they had a decent view of the radio tent. Immediately they were disappointed. Lantern light from inside the tent cast the shadow of Harvey Sims as he sat hunched over his equipment.

Maddock and Bones settled in to wait. After a while boredom set in, interrupted only by the stings and bites of unseen insects. They watched their surroundings from beneath a shroud of protective plants.

Bones swatted at his neck. "Nothing like hanging around in a thicket with a box full of smallpox while you donate your blood to the local bugs."

Suddenly they heard the thud of footfalls approaching fast from the other side of the ham radio tent. Maddock felt Bones tense, reaching for his knife. But he gripped his shoulder, pushing him down.

"Hold up! Listen."

Bones continued to watch through the gaps in the leaves but remained motionless. Shouted commands of some sort drifted to them in the wind. Then two figures came into view. Even in the dim light, Maddock could see that the man in the lead was Fred Spinney. He was being pushed by another man whom he didn't recognize. As they drew nearer to the tent, Maddock held his breath as he realized that one of them was Asian.

And that he held a handgun locked onto the nape of Spinney's neck.

CHAPTER 23

"Where are the rest of the artifacts?" The man gave Spinney a shove and he fell flat on his stomach. "Tell me!" He stamped his foot on the ground next to Spinney's ear, causing him to flinch.

As Maddock and Bones watched from their concealed location in the foliage, another man came stumbling into the cleared area, also pushed by an Asian man with a firearm. George Taylor staggered forward with the crate from his tent held awkwardly in his arms. His captor waved the gun at him, yelling something, and Taylor dropped to his knees as he set the crate down next to Spinney, who looked at it, and at Taylor, with surprise.

"Why don't we talk about this in camp like civilized men?" Spinney pleaded. "What do you want?"

"We wish to question you two and the rest of your men separately. Mizuhi Development Corporation is the rightful owner of this island and these artifacts. You will tell us where the other items are!"

"I'm telling you," Spinney said, "I already showed you what we brought up!"

"You didn't show us this." The man guarding Spinney kicked the crate next to Taylor's knees.

"I didn't know about that." Spinney looked over at Taylor and glared. "What is it?"

They couldn't see his face, but Taylor's Aussie accent was unmistakable to Maddock and Bones. "It used to contain film. But it's gone. The two new guys must have taken it."

"Film? What film?" Spinney wanted to know.

"Enough!" The gunman watching over Spinney kicked him in the shoulder. "You are hiding artifacts from us. You will tell us where they are!"

No one spoke.

Maddock jumped at the sound of the shot, so unexpected was its report. A puff of coral dust drifted away with the wind where the bullet struck the ground next to Spinney's head.

"You will talk now or die!"

It was Taylor who opened his mouth next. "I don't know where the film is. But I know that there is another crate just like this one. I saw it. No idea what was in it or where it is now. Two of these crates were pulled from the plane."

The Mizuhi man standing over Spinney looked down at him. "Is this true?"

"I don't know! I guess it could be, if my own men were stealing from me!"

A handheld radio was produced by the Mizuhi leader and shortly three more Asian men trooped into the clearing. Each of them carried at least one type of gun.

"Tell us more about these two...*new men*." All of the Mizuhi workers eyed Taylor expectantly.

Taylor sang like a bird, spilling the details of his "arrangement" with Maddock and Bones. However, he switched around a few key details of the story, namely that Maddock and Bones were the ones who had come to him with the idea of making side money by selling the artifacts, particularly the cancelled stamps.

In the foliage, Bones whispered some choice words under his breath.

"Then we have to find these two men!"

"They must still be on the island," Spinney said from his prostrate position. "You destroyed our boat and plane, so they didn't use those to escape, and no one else has been here except you."

"Where do you think they are?"

"They must be in the jungle. Outside of our camp, which you already saw, there are no other facilities on this atoll. Nowhere to hide." Spinney looked right at the clump of undergrowth where Maddock and Bones hid.

"Then we will set the jungle on fire. Smoke them out!"

The man watching Spinney spoke once more into his two-way radio, then said, "The first phase of Mizuhi's island development plan has begun. Are there any other secrets you'd like to tell me?" Spinney cowered under the Japanese man's harsh gaze.

Another Mizuhi man came running up to his colleague and dropped a six-gallon red gas can at his feet. He said something in Japanese.

The Mizuhi leader turned and looked directly at the clump of plant life Maddock and Bones were ensconced inside before turning slowly away toward the end of the jungle. "The jungle begins there?"

"Yes," Spinney said from his place on the ground.

The Mizuhi leader pointed to his man with the gas can, who promptly took it over to the jungle. He opened the lid and began to pour gasoline as he walked in around the periphery of the forest's end. Then he calmly took a lighter from his pocket, first used it to light a cigarette, then torched the earth. The ground and leaves were wet, but with the accelerant the flames found the wood and took hold.

The Mizuhi leader pointed to two of his men. "Station yourselves at the other end of the jungle. Find those men. Find those crates. This is our island...this is our destiny!" His eyes took on a faraway look and Maddock admitted to himself that although he didn't think it was possible to be more self-obsessed than Spinney, this Mizuhi guy was making a good run at it.

Then, to Spinney, the conglomerate leader said: "How much gasoline do you have?"

"Probably another hundred gallons."

One of the Mizuhi men addressed their leader. "It will take all of our men to pour it around the jungle."

"Use all of it!" the leader told his men. "No one hides from me!"

Already the smoke from the fire at the end of the forest nearest them offended their nostrils.

In the bushes, Bones had his dive knife unsheathed and was watching the situation unfold in front of them. The

Mizuhi men all left, heading back toward the camp, leaving Spinney and Taylor behind, lying on the ground.

"Smell that?" Bones twitched his nostrils.

"Jungle is starting to burn."

"Maybe we should have just stayed in the cave."

"Clearing the forest would have made it easier for them to find the cave, though. And we can't see the helo coming from there, if we ever do manage to make contact."

"Is your glass always half empty, Maddock?"

"Only when I've been hunkering down in the bushes for hours with a large, cantankerous Indian..."

The banter continued, the two warriors nearly delirious from fatigue.

They cut the chatter when they saw the Mizuhi leader returning with three of his men, their weapons pointed at the prone forms Spinney and Taylor.

"On your feet!"

The EARHART group men turned their heads to look up at the armed Mizuhi men but otherwise made no moves.

"Where are we going?" Spinney pleaded.

"Get up. Now!"

The leader jabbed his pistol menacingly in Spinney's direction.

"Look, Mr...." Taylor trailed off.

"You will call me Tomoaki."

Spinney's eyes narrowed. "I've seen your name on the lawsuits trying to claim salvage rights to the Electra."

Tomoaki's eyes narrowed. "Then you know I am serious about my goals. I will not give up."

"And I will?" Spinney's eyes seemed to bulge from their sockets.

Tomoaki shrugged. "If you wish to live."

"You lost the lawsuit! You have no right to the airplane or anything else on this island!"

"As I said, Mr. Spinney, I will not give up. Legal recourse has failed me, so now I am left with no choice but to take what I desire by force. You can either help me, and live, or stand in my way and die." He pointed his pistol at

Spinney's forehead. "Your choice?"

The EARHART leader looked up at Tomoaki as he lay in the dirt. "How can I possibly help you at this point anyway? My own people seem to be deceiving me." He shot Taylor a look to kill. "I knew nothing about those crates until just now. I swear it." His gaze bore unflinchingly into the eyes of Tomoaki. He went on before his aggressor could speak.

"And the plane? You blew it over the ledge down there with your stupid whale! It's on the bottom of the abyss, probably broken up into little pieces from bashing around on the way down."

But Tomoaki was no longer listening to him. As Maddock and Bones observed from the stand of foliage, he looked at one of his men and then pointed to the radio tent. The man nodded and then proceeded to walk into the tent with his machine gun at the ready. For the next few minutes they heard the sound of rapid gunfire and the shattering of plastic and metal. The destructive noise overshadowed Spinney and Taylor's protests. In a symbolic act of finality, four of Tomoaki's men cut the support cables for the antenna tower and toppled it to the ground.

In the bushes, Maddock and Bones exchanged worried glances. This development was not good for them, either. With no satellite phone and now no radio equipment, how were they going to make that extraction call?

CHAPTER 24

Maddock resisted the urge to swat a fly off his arm. The slightest movement of the bushes could tip off Tomoaki or one of his men, and they'd be finished. Two men, even SEALs, armed with only knives couldn't hope to be a match for what looked like dozens of men with automatic weapons.

"We already issued our press releases and reports of criminal activity hours ago." Spinney somehow managed to sound smug even while face down in the dirt.

"This atoll will be crawling with people any minute!" Carlson added, his voice shaky.

Tomoaki ignored them and beckoned one of his associates. He huddled in close conference with the man for a few seconds until his employee nodded and trotted off toward the camp. Then he pointed his pistol once again at Spinney's head.

"Get up! Both of you! I will not say it again."

Spinney and Carlson struggled slowly to their feet, Spinney slapping Carlson away once when their arms tangled.

"March! That way." Tomoaki pointed with the hand not holding his gun toward the beach on the other side of camp.

"What are we doing?" Spinney's voice had a demanding tone. He stood in place.

Maddock couldn't hear the reply, but it was galvanizing whatever it was, because Spinney and Carlson started trooping down the path toward camp. They were flanked on either side by men with automatic rifles. Tomoaki looked around for a few seconds, taking in the destroyed radio tent, the burning jungle, his men leading the EARHART leaders away. Then he stared directly into the tangle of fern, myrtle, and fire plants, where Maddock and Bones hid. The two SEALs held their breath until Tomoaki turned around and strode after Spinney and Carlson.

Bones looked at Maddock. "Now what?"

Maddock eyed the radio tent. There was a clear path to it for them now, but after the destruction they'd witnessed, the chances of finding a working long distance transmitter were heartbreakingly low.

"Not worth the risk to even check the radio tent."

Bones nodded. "That guy went all postal on it. And even if one of the shortwave units did still work, the antenna's knocked over and there's no way we could get that up without anybody noticing. So how do we contact base?"

Maddock looked toward the jungle, where the blaze was stronger now. Acrid smoke penetrated their stand of foliage. "I doubt it's worth it to snoop around camp looking for a sat-phone someone left behind. Spinney's sat-phone was probably already confiscated or destroyed by Mizuhi, anyway. Let's follow that Tomoaki guy and see where they're taking Spinney and Carlson."

Bones pulled a branch out of the way of his broad shoulders and adjusted his footing. "What about the crate?" He gently patted the box beside them in the foliage.

"Gotta leave it here. At least I have the photos in my pack, though."

"Yeah, even you should be able to handle the weight of a bunch of celluloid. But seriously, we can't take that crate with us. But if we leave it here...what if it burns?"

Maddock contemplated this for a moment. He wondered if the smallpox would be spread if the fire were to crack the porcelain containers open. If there were spores that could be carried by the wind all over the island, or even worse, to the neighboring islands. It was not something he wanted to dwell on. "Then we lose, Bones, and the Navy loses. We need to be light on our feet while we find a way out of here. That's all there is to it. If we can make contact with the extraction team, then we have a chance to come back here for the other half of the goods." He hesitated before adding, "If Mizuhi's men don't find them first. That's the other possibility."

Bones looked out into the smoldering jungle. "Looks like our chances of a successful mission are going up in smoke." He looked over at the crate, and back to Maddock. "For now at least, they're looking in the jungle, toward the cave. So let's do this before Spinney gets out of sight."

Maddock and Bones slipped from the foliage. Both had smeared their faces with mud while in hiding to keep light from reflecting off their skin, but even so, they knew they had to move with a high degree of stealth. The fire created a lot of light, in addition to the powerful search beams and flashlights Mizuhi used to penetrate the darkness, looking for the two men who had disappeared with two of Amelia Earhart's strongboxes. The island was crawling with men who were overzealous about controlling this piece of coral even though it now lacked the legendary pilot's airplane.

He and Bones crept past the rest of the sleep tents, all either unoccupied or burned, until they reached a break in the line of plants they'd been following. From here an exposed path cut directly through the main camp.

"There goes Spinney." Bones followed Maddock's pointing finger just in time to see Spinney disappear on the far side of the camp around the path that led to the beach. In the camp, they could see two Mizuhi men standing and conversing, one of them pointing toward the jungle. Although Maddock and Bones couldn't see them, there were other men still in camp as evidenced by silhouetted figures inside lantern-lit tents and bursts of arguing, some of it in English, some in Japanese. He guessed that some of them were Spinney's men who had already been searched, stripped of any weapons, and left behind to bicker amongst themselves about the invasion.

Maddock removed a shoe and held it up for Bones to see. The big Indian nodded and removed his footwear as well, holding it in one hand. They waited a minute to see if the two men would stop talking and leave, but they didn't, so Maddock gave the signal to go ahead anyway. They didn't want to lose sight of Spinney.

Now barefoot, Maddock and Bones trod light-footed

across the crushed coral, soundless as they passed through the edge of camp, the burning jungle to their right. Across the camp they could see that the dive tent had been ripped down, the equipment inside destroyed, including the air compressor. There would be no more business as usual here for quite some time, even without the fire.

Maddock felt Bones tap his shoulder and he saw him pointing. Tomoaki's procession trod onto the sandy footpath that led out to the beach. The SEALs followed at a safe distance, keeping Tomoaki's party in visual contact but just out of earshot. Soon they reached the beach and the site of the bombed-out pier.

A small boat lay beached not far ahead of Spinney and Carlson, who were being led at gunpoint by a pair of Tomoaki's men. Another Mizuhi employee waited in the boat, starting up the motor when he saw Tomoaki approaching. Maddock and Bones lay flat on the sand. No point in being seen now; it was obvious what was happening. Spinney and Carlson were being transported by boat...but to where? Another part of the island? Would they be taken to do a night dive on the wreck site, to prove that the plane had gone over the ledge and survey the damage their whale had caused? They waited until the sound of the boat's motor had faded into the distance before standing.

Immediately the boat's purpose and destination became clear. About a mile offshore, the dark outline of the Mizuhi ship was just visible in the moonlight. A single, dim light could be seen on the craft, toward which the smaller vessel made a beeline.

"Dollars to donuts that's a tender vessel taking them out to the ship," Maddock said, looking around the beach to make sure they were still unobserved. So far so good.

"I don't know how we're going to get out there, but that ship's going to have satellite communications, radio, the works." Bones stared out to sea where the small boat churned its way out to the white ship.

"I know how we're going to get out there." Maddock stripped off his shirt and hid it along with his shoes under a clump of shrubs at the edge of the beach. Then he stretched and looked out at the ocean, at the black expanse of water between the edge of the reef and the Mizuhi vessel.

"We swim."

CHAPTER 25

"**Maddock, I'm all** for skinny-dipping on tropical, moonlit beaches, just not with you, okay? Now if it was that nurse who gave us the shots..."

"Stay focused, would you, Bones? It's a long swim out to that ship. At least a mile once we get outside the reef, across open ocean. If you want the drag of a shirt that whole way, that's up to you. The only drag I'm willing to put up with is from this." He patted his dive knife, still worn on a sheath strapped to his left calf, inside the leg to minimize the chances of snagging on something.

Bones tugged off his shirt and hid it in the bushes next to Maddock's. "I thought we were done with long-distance swims when we finished training. Remember that time in BUDS when we swam to the Coronado Islands? Nothing will *ever* be worse than that."

Maddock eyed the faintly lit ship one more time, also tracking the small boat on its way out. "Let's hope you're right," he said, wading into the lagoon. He shuffled his feet in the sand to avoid stepping on a stingray or some other denizen of the sea. Bones followed suit and when they reached water that was chest deep, they prepared to swim.

They took one last survey of their surroundings, allowing their eyes to adjust to the low light away from the burning island. Behind them, they could see no one, hower the jungle was an inferno, burning to the ground island-wide. They could hear unintelligible shouts in the distance. Looking out to sea, they could barely make out the white engine wake of the dinghy transporting Tomoaki, Spinney and Carlson out to the Mizuhi ship. While Maddock studied their target vessel, Bones scanned the sea surface intently.

"I think we're ready," Maddock said in a low voice. "Watch the splashing. We'll case out a boarding opportunity when we get closer. What's the matter?"

He saw that Bones was still staring at the water inside the lagoon. "You mean if we get closer. Because I was thinking, if Shankey is still on patrol..."

"Hopefully he died in the explosion and is down there a mile deep with the Electra."

"Hopefully."

With that, they slipped into the calm water of the lagoon and began to swim. Their approach was not that of a Sunday afternoon exerciser doing splashy race to a swim-line and back. They were used to swimming with gear, at times including heavy automatic rifles, and at the very least a pair of fins, so they expected to be slower than usual, but they had also been trained on swimming without gear when necessary. The need to avoid detection by minimizing splashes had been hard-wired into them. They did not rely solely upon any one stroke, especially not a crawl, but instead employed a combination of techniques that collectively made up what they thought of as the combat swimmer stroke: a mishmash of breaststroke, sidestroke, and freestyle.

The combat swimmer stroke was all about using the limbs to generate propulsion beneath the water to maintain silence and effectiveness, with scissors kicks, glides and breaststroke arm-pulls. Top leg always forward, breaths coming after the arms recover together but in different strokes. The goal was efficiency—moving forward in as few strokes as possible. As they swam, Maddock recalled one of their BUDS instructors counting how many strokes they used to get them across a 50-meter pool. The memory calmed him, and he concentrated on lowering that number as he settled into a quiet, almost relaxing rhythm across the lagoon.

A few minutes later they reached the reef marking the edge of the atoll, where waves broke on razor sharp coral. They treaded water while they picked out a channel with deep enough water to pass through into the open ocean beyond, where their real swim would begin.

Maddock felt a wave break over his head and dove,

taking care not to go too deep and hit the bottom. Bones was not beside him but behind, to make sure they both fit through the narrow passage. At one point Maddock felt his knuckles scrape hard coral, skinning them, but he pushed through and in a few seconds he felt the ocean open up, the water becoming calmer and cooler. He asked Bones if he was okay.

"Just another trip through the spin cycle. Never better."

The island was now an orange line in the distance, rimmed with fire. They set out for Mizuhi's ship, again using the combat swimmer stroke, but with the deeper water they had no concern for hitting bottom and could focus entirely on stealth and efficiency. Thirty minutes of swimming later, they stopped to take their bearings. No doubt the small boat had reached the ship long ago. They didn't look for it, but instead pinpointed the ship's light they had seen earlier. It was still on, and appeared brighter from this distance. They could now distinguish details on the ship, such as the rails, the superstructure with radar and various antennae on top, and the darkened silhouettes of men walking the decks.

Maddock looked but couldn't yet discern a boarding ladder. He knew they were usually to the stern, or rear portion of the ship, though, so he aimed for that and set off again. They had just started moving when Bones said, "Hey!"

"Quiet!" Maddock hissed. "What is it?"

Bones spun around in a circle, eyes scouring the sea surface. "Something touched my leg. My ankle. I felt it. It was hard, and rough like sandpaper."

Just as the word *shark* circled in Maddock's mind, Bones pointed to a dark spot on the water about ten feet to the left of him. "There!"

Maddock looked over in time to see a foot-high dorsal fin slice the surface. "Shark!"

Bones studied the animal. "Sure it's not the pilot whale?"

Maddock looked at the beast again. "Look at the dorsal. Shankey's curled over a little on the top, wasn't so knife-edged."

"Speaking of..." Bones reached down, his head going under water for a second. He reemerged with his dive knife gripped in his right hand. He turned slowly in place, tracking the fish's movements as it circled the pair of swimmers. Maddock also brought his knife to a ready position.

Suddenly the shark darted toward them. Its tail splashed the surface, giving them a sense of its length. "Gotta be ten feet long!" Bones observed. Maddock scanned the ship again.

"I say we just keep going. Ten more minutes of swimming and we'll be there and we can get out of the water."

"You think we can go ten minutes with this thing?" Bones eyed the predator warily.

"I do. Sharks are nocturnal hunters, it's just checking us out. Don't act like prey. Swim strong but don't make any sudden movements or splashes. Keep an eye on it. We'll be okay."

"I'm keeping my knife out."

"Just don't drop it. My guess is we'll need it more once we get aboard the ship." Bones appeared less than convinced as his eyes traced the hunter's path.

When the shark turned into the outer periphery of its arc, Maddock and Bones eased confidently into their combat swim strokes. It was difficult not to keep looking back every few seconds to see where the predator was, but they kept on powering forward. After three minutes Maddock broke out of his stroke to look around but saw no sign of the shark. He quickly resumed his pattern, and five minutes later the ship loomed in front of them.

He could see right away that although many people were aboard, they were not expecting to be attacked. No floodlights illuminated the water around the craft and no sentries kept watch. The crew had run the anchor light to avoid possible collision with other vessels. Nevertheless, it appeared that no one was watching their surroundings with any real care.

"What do you think? Ladder entry?" Bones looked to the rear of the boat where the tender vessel that had transported Spinney and Carlson from the island now hung from a crane over the fantail, or back edge of the ship. Nobody was visible but they could hear voices on the stern deck. Maybe thirty feet toward the bow, an access ladder consisting of a set of metal rungs welded directly to the ship's hull led from the waterline to the deck.

Maddock pointed to the ladder and jerked a thumb downward. They would hold their breaths and swim underwater the rest of the way to the ladder to avoid discovery by anyone who happened to look over the rail. Bones glanced around one more time for the shark—or the whale—but seeing nothing he hyperventilated rapidly, taking three quick breaths and then one deep one. Maddock did the same and then the pair of SEALs slipped beneath the surface.

They kept their eyes open as they swam, although they saw nothing of interest except for the dim outline of the ship itself as they reached its hull beneath the ladder. When they surfaced they were mere feet from the lower rungs. They waited for a few seconds to make sure no one was standing directly above them. Then they both grabbed on to the rungs and hung there in the water, resting before beginning the long climb, about three stories.

After a minute Maddock started up the rungs first.

"Seriously, why do I have to be the one to stare at your fat ass the whole way up," Bones complained.

Maddock held a finger over his lips and continued his ascent. He paid meticulous attention to his hand- and footholds, knowing that a fall would mean a loud splash that would alert the crew to their presence. Maddock reached the top of the ladder and paused two rungs down to listen for deck activity. He had no desire to go waltzing into a group of Mizuhi crewmen taking a smoke break or something like that. Bones crept up the ladder until he was a few steps below Maddock.

Satisfied there was no one in the immediate vicinity,

Maddock topped the ladder, his gaze shifting rapidly around the open deck. He sighted three Asian crewmen at the far end of the deck, huddled over a very large of piece equipment that was covered by a tarp.

Fanning a hand below him as a signal for Bones to board, he dropped onto the deck of Mizuhi's ship without a sound.

CHAPTER 26

Maddock tapped Bones' shoulder and pointed to a pair of lifeboats held up sideways, the bottoms facing out toward the ship's work area. They padded over to them, their bare feet soundless on the ship's surfaced deck. They slid behind one of the boats so that they wouldn't be seen while they worked out a plan.

"Now what?" Bones squinted out at the peek-a-boo view of floodlit work deck they had from behind the lifeboat.

"Only saw three guys out there," Maddock said, cocking his head toward the deck. "Which means there must be some action going on inside. They may be interrogating Spinney and Carlson somewhere in there."

Bones' eyes widened at the implication. "Would Mizuhi torture them to get information about what had happened to the artifacts recovered from the plane? Seems extreme."

"Who can say? They've taken Spinney and Carlson this far."

"Our objective now is to make contact with our support," Bones reminded.

Maddock nodded. "I say we scout the ship for a sat-phone, which probably involves breaching the radio room. Then, once we make contact, we do what we can for Spinney and Carlson while we wait for pickup."

Bones nodded, his expression grim. Maddock read his thoughts. The radio room on almost all ships was basically part of the bridge. It would not be unoccupied. He glanced down at the dive knife strapped to his calf. They were woefully under-armed.

"Maybe we should try to blend in instead of fight our way in."

"How?" Bones asked. "Don't say we're gonna knock 'em out and take their uniforms, okay, because you don't look anything like a Japanese guy."

"Unfortunately, what I had in mind is a little more problematic than that, but it might work."

Bones sighed heavily. "You and your 'just might work,' schemes." He shook his head. "Okay. Lay it on me."

"I don't really like it either, but our situation is SNAFU, wouldn't you say?" Maddock said, using the military acronym used informally to denote iffy situations.

Bones nodded. "Out with it, Maddock. I don't want to go missing along with Amelia Earhart if you get my drift."

"Okay. There are three guys over there. Two of them are brothers."

Bones peeked out at the men gathered next to the covered bundle. His face took on a confused look. "Two of them do look the same, but how do you know? And why the hell does it matter, Maddock?"

"Bear with me. I know they're brothers because when we were hiding in the bushes while they took Spinney and Carlson, I saw Tomoaki call a bunch of his men out by name when he was assigning tasks to them. He called out a bunch of different names and then when he got to those two, he said the same name twice. It was in Japanese, yeah, but I'm sure they're last names."

"So those two have the same last name and so they must be brothers, is that it?"

"And they look an awful lot alike."

Bones stared at his friend for a moment before responding. "Maddock, are you going insane in the membrane? How does this help us? We take out the other guy, and then what happens with the brothers?"

Maddock's tone of voice was matter-of-fact. "We overpower the brothers, tie one of them up, and tell the other one that unless he brings us back a satellite-phone in ten minutes without letting anybody know what's going on, we're going to kill his brother."

Bones rubbed one of his eyes while he contemplated this. After a few seconds he still had said nothing.

"You're speechless?" Maddock knew it was beyond rare

for the outgoing Indian to have nothing to say.

But then Bones looked up and said, "What if you're wrong and they're not really brothers? No offense, but your Japanese is probably not what it should be."

"Are you saying I'm not a cunning linguist?"

"That's what she said."

"Even if they're not actually brothers, the plan could still work just based on friendship and camaraderie. Not wanting to get their fellow crewman killed."

Bones looked up for a moment. "I doubt that'd work if the shoe was on the other foot and it was us over there." He nodded toward the deck. Maddock shook his head and then Bones spoke again.

"We better get going before those guys go somewhere else or more people come out."

By this point in their careers together, Maddock had a lot of respect for Bones, respect born of a slew of close calls and hairy situations the world over, and that respect just crept up another notch. He was asking a lot with this plan, and not a lot of guys, even SEALs, would go along so willingly with something that could turn sour in so many ways.

"Right." Maddock snapped to attention, realizing that it was game on. Bones was one hundred percent correct: the situation was fluid and they needed to do this fast, before it changed.

Maddock crept to the edge of the lifeboat and peered out on the work deck. One of the men—one of the *brothers*, he told himself—was hunched over the tarp, either tying or untying it by the looks of things. The other two men appeared to be arguing, gesticulating as they stood and talked.

Knives drawn, the two SEALs belly-crawled out from under the lifeboat onto the deck. Maddock pointed to the left side of the tarp, then tapped his chest, then pointed to the right and tapped Bones. They would split up, going around opposite ends of the covered equipment, meeting in the middle at their targets.

Maddock had the simpler, more direct route, but also the more open one. Bones had farther to go and would have to step over obstacles—piles of electrical cables and rope on deck, head-high spools of chain and 55-gallon steel fuel drums, but these things would also provide him with some cover.

They heard the voices of the three Mizuhi employees burst into laughter. Over what, they didn't know, but they were glad they were distracted, at least for the moment. Maddock gave Bones the signal and they set out on their respective routes.

Bones had just slid into position behind the drums when he heard the metallic *clang* of a door slamming shut from somewhere above, up in the superstructure. He froze in place, noting that their targets did not stop talking. He looked over to make eye contact with Maddock but he had no line of sight. Maddock was still hunkered down behind the left end of the tarp bundle as far as he knew. Looking up, he watched a hard-hatted crew member pass along a walkway without looking down until he rounded the corner and kept going toward the front of the ship.

Bones saw one of the brothers showing some kind of electronic device to the other two, and as they leaned in to look at it the naval warrior dashed to the right-side end of the covered object. He knelt, trying to keep his breathing shallow and quiet while he looked up at the walkway where the other crewman had appeared. He didn't like this vantage point. If anyone were to walk around that corner up there, he was in direct line-of-sight.

Bones lowered his head to the deck before peeking around the corner to get a fix on the targets. If they happened to be glancing his way he needed as low a profile as possible. In the past he'd worked with small dental style mirrors for the purpose of seeing around corners, and he wished he had one now, but he would have to make do. Thrusting his head out just enough to see beyond the tarp, he saw the three men standing about twenty feet from him, a little closer to Maddock's end. And there was Maddock, crouched and ready, already making his move, prowling toward the men.

He motioned to Bones.

Go!

The big Indian sprang, knife in his right hand, more for the intimidation factor than to actually use it. He knew that he and Maddock would have little trouble dispatching these three unsuspecting men with their bare hands. But in his business, it didn't pay to get complacent, and right now overall, the odds were definitely stacked against them.

Right away Bones could see his target. The man who was not one of the brothers was both taller and chunkier, and standing closer to Bones to boot. He would take him down first, leaving the two brothers to Maddock until he could assist. He hoped that Maddock would be okay with this, since right now they had no way to communicate anything of that complexity.

With his bare feet, his track-runner start off the line was silent and he wasn't noticed until he was mere feet away and coming at a sprint. He launched himself into the tallest man, using the steel butt of the dive knife to strike him with non-lethal force in the head. The crewman was unconscious before he hit the deck. His spindly limbs were wrapped around Bones' body, though, and the wily Cherokee had no choice but to go down with his victim. He saw three pairs of legs engaged in a struggle above him. Maddock had arrived.

Bones rolled the tall guy off of him and shot to his feet. Maddock was grappling with the brother who was facing Bones. That man tried to warn his twin, who stood with his back to Bones, by uttering something in Japanese. It was too late. Bones wrapped his arms around the much smaller man, the left gripping his abdomen like a vice, the right clutching the knife blade in front of his throat.

Maddock had his knife sheathed had full control of the other brother, bear-hugging him into submission. He cocked his head toward the lifeboats. Bones took his meaning immediately. They needed cover. Right now before anyone saw them.

"Speak English?" Maddock hissed at his captive.

"Some." He trembled in Maddock's grasp, the suddenness of the attack having unnerved him.

"Stay quiet and do what we say and you will all live. Do you understand?"

The man nodded feverishly. "Yes, understand. What you want?"

"We're going to those lifeboats over there, and then we'll tell you. Don't resist, and this will all be over soon without anyone getting hurt."

The Japanese man looked extremely confused, but nodded. Bones lifted the tarp a little and rolled the tall, unconscious crewman under it. He used his knife to slice a length of cord that had been tying the tarp down and put it in his pocket. Then he and Maddock each gripped one of the brothers and escorted them at a trot to the lifeboats.

Once ensconced beneath the small boats, Maddock and Bones had the two brothers sit cross-legged on the deck. Maddock addressed them.

"We require use of a satellite phone. Where is the nearest one located?"

The two brothers looked at one another.

"Seriously, Maddock? They barely speak English." Bones held a hand up to the side of his head, miming talking on a telephone. "Phone," he said.

The captives nodded in unison.

"Where!" Maddock brandished his knife.

"Bridge," one of the brothers said.

"Tomoaki," the other said almost at the same time.

"Which is it?" Maddock hissed.

"Both!" the brother sitting next to Bones said. "Tomoaki has one. Captain has one on bridge."

"Would it be unusual for either of you to walk into the bridge and request to borrow the sat-phone?" Maddock pressed.

The brothers looked at one another and one gave a shrug. "We are machine fabricators."

Bones looked at Maddock. "I take that as a 'yes'."

But then one of the brothers looked up at Maddock, nodding. "Can say I need call Tokyo to confirm parts order."

Maddock nodded at him. "Good." Then he indicated for Bones to tie the other brother's hands behind his back.

"What are you doing?" the brother who had just spoken said.

"Get the phone. Bring it back. Tell no one. Understand?" Bones hoped the glare he directed at the man was sufficiently intimidating.

The Japanese crewman appeared confused.

"Do you understand?" Bones repeated.

The man pointed at his trussed brother. "He come with me?"

Maddock and Bones both shook their heads. Maddock brought the knife near the brother's neck. He looked the Japanese man in the eyes while Bones made a show of cinching down his brother's restraints.

"You have five minutes to bring that satellite phone back here without alerting anyone." Bones held up his hand fingers and thumb spread apart.

"After five minutes, if we still don't have a working sat-phone, your brother here will die." Maddock showed the man his watch and then made a slashing motion with the knife in the air in front of his brother's neck. "Are we clear?"

The unbound brother nodded, eyes wide. He looked at his brother, said something in Japanese, then said to Maddock, "Five minutes. I go now."

He got up and crawled out from the boat, looking back once before standing and walking briskly away.

"I hope," Bones said, watching the man walk away, "he likes his brother better than my sister likes me."

CHAPTER 27

"I wonder what's under that tarp," Bones said, while he, Maddock and their captive waited under the lifeboat. Thankfully the Japanese man had remained quiet and compliant thus far. Maddock tapped him and pointed out to the tarp-covered bundle.

"What's under the tarp?"

The man made a grunting noise while he looked out at the tarp, and then seemed to lose interest. "Airplane."

Bones looked at Maddock, then back to the captive. "Airplane? What kind?"

Having another way out of here was a possibility they hadn't considered.

"There's no way even the smallest of planes could take off from this ship," Maddock pointed out.

"Unless it's a float plane." Bones' suggestion piqued Maddock's interest as he mentally pictured the airplanes with pontoons instead of wheels that could land and take off on water, like the one that had been destroyed at the pier. He looked at their prisoner. "What type of plane is it?"

The captive shook his head. "It no work. Just model."

Maddock and Bones exchanged quizzical glances. "Model of what?" Maddock pressed.

The crewman shrugged. "Old plane. You go see." He pointed over at the tarp. Bones looked that way with interest.

"Don't." Maddock looked at Bones, shaking his head. "Not worth the risk. We hunker down here until he's back with the sat-phone."

Bones made a mock sad face. "But it's a plane, Maddock."

"A model."

Bones eyed the captive doubtfully. "Not that I think this guy would ever lie to us...but there's kind of a language barrier at play here. Maybe he doesn't mean the word 'model' like the way we think of 'model'."

"How else would he think of it?" Maddock glanced at his watch.

"I don't know, model, like really good? A *model* plane, as in one that all other planes look up to?"

Maddock muttered something incomprehensible under his breath.

"It's okay, we can just sit here and wonder..." Bones glanced longingly out at the tarp-covered plane.

"You know the price if you get spotted."

"I won't be spotted. Besides, it's getting a little hot in here, some fresh air will keep me alert for when it's time to move."

"Go, then."

Bones crouched at the entrance to their hideout, scoping out the work deck. Satisfied the coast was clear, he made a silent, nimble dash to the end of the tarp where Maddock had waited before. He undid one of the tie-downs and slid beneath the tarp. Beneath it he found that it was dim but he could still see in the bluish light from the work deck's floodlights penetrating the fabric.

Immediately he could make out that he was in the presence of a large, metal machine. He reached out a hand and ran it along the smooth metal of a...wing! Looking back for confirmation, he nodded to himself as he recognized a tail section. Then, up front, the fuselage tapered into a rounded nose. What's more, Bones realized, this was no modern aircraft. In fact...his mouth dropped open as he processed the unbelievable.

He was looking at a Lockheed Electra airplane. It couldn't be Earhart's, though. He'd personally witnessed it slide into the abyss. Plus, this one was in pristine condition, looking as though it had never even spent time in the air, much less underwater. He gazed in wonder along its length.

Then what the heck was it?

Bones recalled the Mizuhi crewman's words. *No work,*

just a model. He decided to confirm that for himself. He crept beneath the wing over to where it joined the body of the plane, where one of the twin turboprop engines were. It had a propeller, he could see that much even in the weak ambient light. He wished he had a flashlight to peer into the engine's innards to see if it had actual parts or was just an empty shell, as the crewman had suggested. It looked real enough from the outside in this poor light, but he wasn't about to start prying panels open.

He listened for a few seconds to make sure all was silent out on deck, and then slinked back toward the tail section. He passed the supine body of the man he had knocked unconscious and stopped to check his pulse. Still alive. He continued on to the tail section. There was a small tear in the tarp overhead here, and a little more light came through. Enough for him read the serial number painted on the tail.

NR 16020.

The same as Amelia Earhart's!

Bones was confused. Here was a plane that looked exactly like Earhart's Electra, even down to the serial number. He wasn't sure which exact model it was, but it sure looked a lot like the one they had found underwater, and yet there was no way it could be the one they had found underwater.

*A model...*He reflected on the crewman's words again, then on the fireside conversation in Spinney's camp about how Mizuhi wanted to turn the island into a resort based on Earhart's plane...

And then Bones heard a noise.

Not human. Machine. He laid a hand flat on the deck and felt the vibration. The ship's engines were starting up! A few seconds later, a second sound came—the grating of metal on metal, which Bones recognized as the ship's anchor being hauled back in. They were getting underway.

Not sure what that could mean since it was still the middle of the night, Bones decided it was time to get back to Maddock and their captive. He stayed underneath the tarp while he walked back along the plane's length to the nose, the end closest to where they hid under the lifeboat. He had just gripped the bottom of the tarp to lift it high enough to slip under when he heard voices approaching on the work deck.

Not Maddock's.

Cursing lightly under his breath, he let the tarp drop back into position and retreated from the edge. The men he could hear spoke in Japanese, so he had no idea what they were saying, but they didn't sound angry. They sounded industrious, though, like they had a job to do and they were getting it done.

Bones froze in place as he heard the sound of the rumpling tarp from over by the tail section as someone started to pull it up. A sliver of artificial light tracked toward him. Realizing that the tarp was being removed, Bones knew he had to do something. If he simply remained standing here he would be seen in a few more seconds when the tarp was removed.

He looked around the deck beneath the plane. Saw no recourse of any kind. He considered slipping out from under the tarp and making a dash for it somewhere else on the deck, perhaps to the lifeboat, but from the sound of the voices around, there were far too many men in his midst to give that any chance of success. The tarp began to slide from the plane.

Then Bones looked up. The model plane's cockpit was directly above him. He moved to the base of the cockpit where the step ladder was and climbed. He saw the shadow of a man duck underneath the tarp by the tail of the plane to help pull it off, and prayed there was a real cockpit and not some filled-in space. He topped over the edge of the cockpit on the ladder and was relieved to see there was in fact a deep cockpit.

Bones flopped into it without making any noise, just before the rest of the tarp was pulled away from the plane. The inside of the cockpit was flooded with light. Fortunately, the only way a man could see into it was if he climbed up into it as Bones had done, or if he was looking down from above.

Bones took a glance at the controls and smiled. They weren't real gauges, just little plastic discs with numbers painted on them. The Japanese guy was right. This was just a life-size model of a plane—of Amelia Earhart's Electra. Bones curled up on the floor of the cockpit, making himself as small as possible, which wasn't easy with his size.

He heard men walk nearby, then retreat. Shortly after that, he felt the model plane begin to roll.

The plane was being moved.

CHAPTER 28

Maddock put a hand on the Japanese crewman's shoulder. *Don't move.* He mentally kicked himself for allowing Bones to investigate what was under the tarp. Now they were in one hell of a situation. He counted six Mizuhi men moving the uncovered plane along the deck. Where was Bones? And, he couldn't help but notice in spite of the situation: the plane looked exactly like Earhart's Electra! He checked his watch: fourteen minutes had passed and still the brother had not returned.

The crewman captive's eyes grew wide upon seeing Maddock look at his watch. He shook his head rapidly. "No, no! Wait, wait! He will come!"

Like it or not, Maddock didn't see what other choice he had at the moment. They were no longer alone on deck, and Bones was missing... or was he? Maddock thought about it as he peered out from beneath the lifeboat. The men didn't have him. He was beneath the tarp when they first came out...He supposed it was possible Bones made a run for it when the tarp came off, but then wouldn't he have run here, under the lifeboat? Maybe not if he thought it would also give up Maddock's cover. Or, Maddock realized, watching the big model wheel across the deck, maybe Bones was *in* the plane? In the cockpit? It was possible. The more he thought about it, it seemed *probable* compared to the other possibility that Bones had run off to another part of the ship. He would have had very little time to make a decision, and from his place under the tarp, running out from under it would be pretty much of a crapshoot as to whether he was spotted.

And what of the brother sent to fetch the sat-phone? Could these men on deck now be part of a response triggered by alerting Tomoaki that the two Americans were holding his brother hostage? Or did he simply need this much time to locate it and return here? These thoughts swirled in Maddock's brain like a maelstrom while he stared out from behind the lifeboat, wondering what his next move was going to be. He might be able to sneak around the ship himself, employing stealth moves, but with his captive? No way. He'd have to leave him behind, and with no one brandishing a knife at his side, he doubted he'd stick around.

What's it going to be, Maddock?

But then his choice was made for him.

The Japanese captive, keenly aware that Maddock was preoccupied with watching the activity on deck and lost in thought, suddenly shot backward—toward the opening away from the main activity on deck, away from where Maddock watched. Even though his hands were tied, he was able to scoot backward rapidly until his body was outside of the lifeboat before Maddock could stop him. Maddock reached out and grabbed one of his ankles but it was too late.

The man yelled at the top of his lungs. Something in Japanese, but Maddock knew it didn't matter what it was. The crew on deck heard it and two of them came running to check it out. Maddock was about to be found out. He told himself in a fleeting thought just before he bolted that at least he'd be drawing attention away from Bones in the plane. If in fact that's where he was.

And then he was off like a shot from a low crouch, track-runner style, a backpack-wearing, shirtless sprinter with a knife strapped to his calf, racing along the side of the work deck. He briefly considered that he could dive over the rail and hide in the water, but then dismissed the idea out of hand. What good would that do Bones or the mission? He not only had to escape, but live to return the requested materials to his commander. That's what he was here for and that's what he would do, or die trying. He had no doubt that in his position, Bones would do the same for him.

He was surprised to hear no gunshots by the time he reached a narrow gangway that led to a different section of the ship. Footsteps pounded after him on the metal deck and then the gangway. They were right behind him, now.

And then shouting, in Japanese, but he was surprised to also recognize an English word: *Stop!*

The ship's rail still on his left and only a row of portholes to his right, Maddock had no choice other than to keep running the length of the gangway, his bare feet pounding the metal walkway mesh, his footfalls echoing against the side of the steel ship.

The end of the gangway opened onto a semi-enclosed area with several doorways off to the right. Maddock slowed for a couple of seconds, picked a door and ran for it, hearing the man behind him nearing the end of the gangplank. Maddock got to the door and reached for the handle. It swung open at the same time, a short but burly Mizuhi crewman bursting out of it. His eyes opened wide at the sight of the intruder. He groped for his sidearm, a pistol Maddock recognized as a Korean-made K5 9mm. He held the crewman's right hand in a vice grip with one hand while he used the other to draw his dive knife.

Maddock brought the butt of the knife up in a swift hammering motion to the underside of his foe's chin. He heard his teeth knock together and then the man fell backward. Maddock was on him in a flash, knocking him in the head again with the knife butt, taking the K5 as it slipped from his now relaxed hand as the man slumped into the doorway.

The two crewmen from the work deck on Maddock's heels stood down when they saw Maddock take possession of the firearm. Neither of them were armed. Apparently Tomoaki separated his soldiers from his workmen. Maddock had no time to reflect on this, however, as he backpedaled through the open door.

A tight, ladder-like staircase led up, while a dead-end room opened up in front of him, housing a series of pumps and switches. He looked up the stairs, saw no one up there and leapt onto the rung-like steps, hauling himself up. He came out on a long, narrow hallway with metal doors closed on either side. No people in sight. Below him he heard the crackle of a two-way radio and knew he didn't have long before reinforcements arrived.

None of the doors had windows set into them, nor could he hear anything behind them. About halfway down the hall, with the first man behind him about to top the ladder, he tried a door to his left. Locked. Tried another, this time on the right. Also locked. He didn't have time to wonder what was behind them. Kept going, hands flying out to pull on handles as he went...finally, near the end of the hall, with a man cautiously approaching behind him, Maddock turned a handle and a door opened.

A machine shop. Grinders, table saws, lathes, and a host of other tools he was not familiar with. But he recognized it as a dangerous place to be in a fight. He also recognized that there was a door on the far side of the room. He ran through the shop, dodging between workbenches and equipment. He flipped a switch on a table saw as he went by and was pleased to hear it start buzzing, creating a noise screen as he ducked and wheeled across the room.

Maddock slipped out and shut the door just as his pursuers entered the workroom. He looked around at his new surroundings. He was in an open area with a staircase leading up to the ship's main superstructure, and another down to a gangway on the opposite side of the ship from the one he'd been on to get here. Presumably it also led back to the work deck.

He was not alone here.

Two crewmen stood in conference at the foot of the stairs. He didn't recognize them. They turned and saw him walk into the space, then did a double-take, one of them reaching for a pistol in a holster at his waist. Maddock raised his new K5.

"Freeze! Drop the gun!" Maddock knew there was a good chance they didn't understand English, or most of it, but at the same time was pretty sure the meaning was universal.

The unarmed man put his hands up high immediately. The one with the gun hesitated, then raised his hands slowly. When his hands were extended halfway up, he moved suddenly, aiming the gun at Maddock. The SEAL fired his 9mm, hitting his opponent in the wrist, right where he'd aimed. The gun was knocked from his grasp and clattered to the floor where it skidded to a stop not far from the two crewmen.

Neither made a move for it. Blood dripped onto the gray-painted floor from the hand of the man Maddock had wounded.

Then the door to the area opened and the two men in pursuit of Maddock burst out of the workroom, shouting at the sight of the confrontation. Maddock bolted up a staircase that switch-backed up the side of the hulking superstructure, knowing the two men behind him were unarmed or they'd have shot him already. He kept his pistol pointed down as he climbed, wanting to keep them unarmed for as long as possible.

He made it up one level and passed a door there, deciding he wanted more distance between himself and those chasing him. Up another level, leg muscles burning with the effort, flashing on his SEAL training and how all the brutal exercises now made perfect sense to him. He heard the metal rungs below him reverberate with the footfalls of the men after him, and then, much closer, felt the vibration as the door he had just passed slammed shut. Two more crewmen had just emerged from it and started up after Maddock. From the multiple whistles and pings of close-by rounds whizzing around his head and ricocheting off a metal railing, Maddock knew that this pair was armed. And they had orders to kill.

One flight further up he ducked into what looked to be a break room; a billiards table occupied the center of the space, vending machines lined the walls, and a muted television hung in a corner playing a Japanese baseball game. There was another door on the opposite side of the room and Maddock ran to it, wanting to make sure he wasn't boxed in. It opened onto an upper walkway overlooking the main deck three flights below. He left the door wide open, went back into the rec room and grabbed a pool cue from a rack on the wall.

He ducked behind the pool table, willing himself to silence his labored breathing. He squeezed the pistol, feeling its weight. He hoped he wouldn't need to use it again, but at the same time knew he had to be ready. As expected, the two gun-toting crew members were first into the room, but Maddock knew the two unarmed ones couldn't be far behind. He wielded the cue like a bat from his kneeling position, and heard the two men shout something when they saw the open door.

Maddock swung the fat end of the pool stick into the knees of the first gunman as he ran past the end of the pool table. He went down with a shriek of pain, causing the man right behind him to trip over him and go down also. As they lay there in a tangled heap, Maddock used his pool stick to knock the guns out of each of their hands. He hooked one through the trigger guard with the stick and flipped it onto the pool table where it landed halfway into a side pocket.

"Nine-millimeter, side pocket!" Maddock couldn't resist, plucking it out and tucking it into the front waistband of his shorts while he covered the aggressors with his K5.

He slid the other gun across the floor toward his intended exit, ran to it and picked it up. Carrying three pistols on the run without a holster seemed careless and probably unnecessary, although he would like to give one to Bones if he got the chance, but he definitely didn't see the need to leave it behind for them to use on him again, either. Nor did he want to take the time to put it into his pack. Eyeing the dark ocean over the side of the ship as he emerged out of the break room onto the upper walkway, he did a double-take. The ship was moving. Maddock threw one of the weapons overboard, leaving him armed with matching K5s, so much the better for dual-wielding should it come to that.

Back in the room he heard the first pair of crew find their associates on the floor, a loud verbal exchange ensuing. Maddock moved fast along the walkway, trying to look ahead as he went. To the right was only a long drop to the deck and ocean just beyond that, while to the left ran the steel side of the superstructure, a couple of doorways set into it up ahead. Beyond that, the walkway descended in stair-step fashion to the deck.

He glanced back but didn't see anyone following him yet. He supposed that, having been disarmed, they knew he now had control of up to three guns, and for them discretion was the better part of valor. He continued to slink along the walkway until he reached the first of the two doors. It was locked, but a small porthole set into the door revealed a fluorescent-lit room that looked to Maddock's cursory glance like a spartan office, all folding furniture and bare walls but for a single, blank whiteboard. No one was inside.

He decided to keep moving. He reached the second door set into the wall on his left, just before the walkway led into a descending staircase. He could hear people down on the main deck but not see them. He was so intent on listening to the far-away activity he almost failed to notice that the door next to him was ajar. Instinctively, Maddock crouched down low and leaned in closer to the open gap into the room.

This one was not empty. Inside, Tomoaki paced the length of a table while he yelled at the two men seated at it. Two guards with automatic rifles stood guard behind him. And, seated at the table, where a large satellite photo print of the island lay spread out before them, Fred Spinney yelled while Steve Carlson pointed dramatically at a forested area.

"They must have hidden them in there somewhere!" He poked the map for emphasis. "That's where I'd look for those crates, if you idiots haven't burned them up already."

Tomoaki's features contorted into a mask of rage and he moved toward Spinney, gun in hand. Maddock shrank back from the door, weapon ready but held down. If Tomoaki was going to shoot Spinney, he would have to intervene. Distaste for the egocentric expedition leader aside, he could not stand still and watch while another human being was executed. But then Tomoaki shifted the gun's grip in his hand, holding it barrel first. Maddock maintained his stance, watching as Tomoaki pistol-whipped Spinney in the head.

CHAPTER 29

Maddock withdrew from the slightly open door. He was pretty sure he hadn't been spotted and the men seemed unaware that shots had been fired on the ship, but the adrenaline was still surging. From the looks of things, Tomoaki continued trying to get information out of Carlson, information the researcher did not have, but that Maddock did, much of it carried right on his back. Spinney, meanwhile, was still conscious but slumped over on the table, head on his elbows like a sleepy school kid. Except that sleepy school kids did not have blood trickling down their foreheads. Maddock sure as heck did not want to end up sitting at that table next to the EARHART Group men, where would be hated by both parties in the room. At least he was now armed, and with the element of surprise he might even be able to eliminate Tomoaki and his goons with an offensive attack, but if that failed he was ridiculously outgunned.

Instead, he opted for continued stealth in pursuit of a satellite phone. He wasn't looking forward to breaching the radio room, where more machine-gun toting lackeys likely waited, but he was all too aware that as long as they remained aboard, it was only a matter of time before either he or Bones was discovered. Mission success depended on making that sat-phone call.

Maddock slipped very quickly past the door, conscious of the fact that even though he turned his face away as he passed, the sight of a barefoot, shirtless man with a backpack would raise suspicions immediately. He paced down the remainder of the walkway until he reached the stairs leading down, recalling the voices he'd heard just before reaching the room with Spinney and Carlson. But now nothing disturbed the near-silence.

Wait...not silence...a sound. A voice? It was eerie, an

ethereal wail, coming from what sounded like it might be underneath him. He crept down the stairs, head on a swivel, alert for any human presence. The ocean rushed by on his right, the ship now at cruising speed. He wondered fleetingly where they were going, but had no time to ponder it as he reached the bottom of the staircase and looked behind him. A cavern-like space yawned beneath the overhang of the stairs and superstructure above, dominated by a large-diameter pool five feet high above deck, filled with water.

In the pool a black fin sliced through the water. Maddock moved to it for a closer look, noting the single, closed door set into the wall behind it. He moved to one side of the pool so that should someone emerge either out on deck behind him, or out of the door, he could duck behind the pool's side for cover.

He walked up to the edge and peered over. For a moment, he entertained the possibility that this was perhaps a shark, but no...it was a small whale. As if to confirm this fact, the whale exhaled a plume of mist with a breathy gasp.

And not just any whale, Maddock realized, following the animal's circular pattern with his gaze. The black hide, the rounded melon, rows of peg-like teeth...this was a pilot whale. *The* pilot whale, Maddock corrected himself. *Shankey survived the explosion that sent the plane over the ledge!*

Unless they had a second pilot whale? This small holding pen looked barely big enough for one whale, much less two, not that he would hold Mizuhi Corp to high moral standards. But looking closer, Maddock examined the ridges of the dorsal fin. He knew that, much like human fingerprints, dorsal edge patterns were unique to individual whales. He recalled from their close scrapes with Shankey that there was a distinctive triple-notch sculpted out of the top edge of the fin, just below where it curled over. *There it is.* This was definitely Shankey.

Although knifeless at the moment, the whale was currently outfitted with a new explosive. An LED light on the disc-shaped device blinked green, which Maddock knew meant the explosive was not currently armed.

Looking more closely at the tank, Maddock could see that a plastic chute was gated off inside of it. When the gate was lifted, though, he could see that the whale could slide through the tube, which went through the ship's side and overboard. He heard the ship's engines change in pitch. The motion of the vessel changed, too, becoming more rocky as it slowed. Cautiously, Maddock moved to the rail near the opposite side of the tank so that he could look off the ship. Expecting to see only choppy, open ocean, he had to make himself look twice at the land mass now not far in front of him, brimmed with orange fire.

The atoll!

They floated just outside the calm waters of the lagoon. *What are we doing back here?* Maddock wondered if it meant that Tomoaki had gleaned information he found to be promising from Spinney and Carlson regarding the location of the crate. He tried to suppress his nerves as he speculated as to whether the Mizuhi team sweeping the island may have come across their smallpox crate hidden in the foliage. That would be extremely problematic. Hopefully Tamoaki was just pursuing some wild goose chase given to him by Spinney and Carlson.

One thing was clear. Something was going on with the ship, and so he and Bones needed to regroup. With any luck, Maddock reflected, already moving away from the pool toward the open deck, at least some of the crew would leave the ship for the island, giving them better odds at overcoming the remaining crew while they searched for a sat-phone. He should have Bones with him, anyway, to breach the radio room and bridge areas. He could give him one of the K5s and then they would be much more effective than they were now, split and with one of them weaponless.

He began carefully making his way back to the work deck, the last place he saw Bones. One thing that gave him hope was that, if he had been captured, he probably would have been in that room with Tomoaki and the EARHART men, if he had been. Maddock could only hope he was still at large as he snuck under a stairwell landing and waited for two crewmen to walk past. When it was clear he dashed to the base of a large crane, hiding behind it while scoping out the next leg of his progress. In such a fashion he worked his way toward the stern of the ship, occasionally dodging crewmen, staying out of sight, until at last he was overlooking the work deck.

What he saw made him catch his breath.

The life-size model Electra was now clutched in the jaws of a massive crane, swinging a few feet over the deck as it swayed gently. He didn't know what they planned to do with it, but that wasn't his concern. What did cause him anxiety was his view of the cockpit.

Bones lay curled in a ball on the floor of the fake plane.

From his hiding spot behind a boxy air handler tucked back beneath a stairwell, Maddock took in his surroundings. Perhaps a dozen men now occupied the work deck, most of them highly focused on tasks related to moving the plane. Maddock watched as one of the men, seated at a control station for the crane, began to move his hands over its controls.

The crane began to move, carrying the replica airplane with it. He saw Bones stir within the plane but still make no move to sit up.

Don't get up now, Bones, they'll see you. He knew it must be difficult for Bones to resist the urge to get a visual on his situation.

Maddock didn't see how he was going to get Bones out of that plane without anyone knowing. Even with his twin K5s there was no way he could hold off that many of them. And he couldn't be sure yet, but what were they doing with the model—preparing to lower it over the side into the water? What for?

And then he recalled the talk of Mizuhi's development goals, how they wanted to turn the island into a profitable luxury mega-resort, complete with Amelia Earhart's airplane and fancy bungalows dotting the beach. Maddock scratched his head in wonderment. It seemed that when faced with the fact that they were unable to scare the EARHART Group off so that they could lay claim to the island, Mizuhi had made the horrible executive decision to simply take over the atoll by sheer brute force. He took advantage of the island's remoteness and essentially kicked off the atoll's sole occupants to begin construction of their new paradise. They had already started burning down the jungle, Maddock thought, watching the island burn to his left, the smell of smoke hanging sharply in the night air. And now they were about to drop a full-scale model of Earhart's Electra into the atoll's lagoon, probably to dupe unsuspecting tourists into believing they'd found the real thing! Probably so that tourists could snorkel on it.

Maddock thought fast, clutching one of his two pistols. As soon as they lowered that plane into the water, Bones would be seen by the crew. The situation was rapidly getting out of control. He had to do something, but saw only near-suicidal options. He looked around the ship, at the crew on deck working the plane, saw a few more men streaming onto the work deck, a couple leaving the deck to climb into the superstructure. He needed a major distraction of some sort. Looking over at the burning atoll, he was discouraged. If that wasn't distraction enough, what could he possibly do to provide one?

One of the men on deck shouted at the crane operator to do something and Maddock saw the plane spinning, with Bones inside, twirling in place as it hung suspended over the deck. He wasn't sure if they intended to drop it into the lagoon from here, or wanted to get it onto the island itself. Either way, as soon as they lowered it Bones would be spotted. There was no way Maddock would be able to get Bones out of there without getting both of them killed. *SNAFU.* The situation was so bad, it seemed insurmountable. The ship was too big and had too many crew to be able to locate a sat-phone in a practical amount of time. He shook his head in disgust at their early optimism. Ridiculous. Now they were in a serious pickle that nothing short of a disaster affecting the ship itself would be able to...

A disaster affecting the ship itself...

A devilish grin materialized on Maddock's face as he stared out over the busy work deck. He banished the phrase *long-shot* from his brain. Something had to be done.

Hang in there Bones. He chuckled to himself as he glanced at the special warfare operator spinning slowly in the suspended model plane before turning and running back the way he had come.

CHAPTER 30

Maddock retraced his steps carefully back the way he had come, careful not to let his enthusiasm for trying out his new plan overcome his operational judgment. He still had to be extremely wary. Ducking, watching, listening nearly every step of the way. The entire mission was on the line, not to mention his and Bones' personal safety. He hung cat-like from the underside of a stairwell while a crewman ran up it, oblivious to his presence. When the man was out of sight, Maddock dropped to the deck and made the final dash to his destination.

The whale's pool.

Shankey glided silently through another of his endless circles, the water barely rippling with his motion. Maddock glanced around the area beneath the overhang, took a deep breath and approached the pool. He couldn't deny that he questioned his ability to do what he was about to try, but if it was successful it would provide just the distraction he was looking for.

Maddock watched Shankey for a moment while he summoned mental images of the Navy marine mammal trainers he'd observed in San Diego. The hand signals they used to interact with their dolphins. He doubted they would be exactly the same as what Mizuhi used with their pilot whale, but hopefully they would be close enough. He knew that the U.S. Navy marine mammal training programs were often emulated around the world because of their stellar reputation.

Hanging from a peg on the wall nearby was a whistle and he grabbed it and looped it around his neck. He knew that it would be easily heard around the ship and that once he used it he would need to be ready to move. But he also knew that much of the handling was done with hand signals alone.

He pressed himself up against the side of the tank and held an arm straight out over the water, palm flat. He was surprised when the whale suddenly altered its course and popped nose-up in the middle of its pool, eyeing Maddock curiously. It was a good sign. Next Maddock balled his outstretched hand into a fist and brought it to his chest. *Come here.*

Shankey dipped beneath the water and in two more seconds appeared in front of Maddock at the edge of the tank, his big head standing higher than Maddock's own. He made a few clicking noises. Maddock made a slow sideways motion with his palm. *Lay down.* The whale eased itself into a prostrate position, floating on its belly in front of Maddock.

The green light on the explosive device blinked on top of Shankey's head. It had been placed there so that the whale could nudge it onto something, as it had attempted with Earhart's plane. But Maddock had a use for it himself. He studied the device's latch mechanism for a moment and then reached out and unsnapped the catch that fastened it to the whale's harness. He felt it click and then he pried the bomb loose from its fitting and took it from the whale.

He watched the LED carefully to make sure its pattern or color hadn't changed. Still blinking green at the same rate. *So far so good.* He patted Shankey's back, telling the animal it had done a good job. Then he looked back down at the explosive device, smiling. He now had a bomb at his disposal, but how to set the timer?

He noticed a raised backplate and found he was able to slide it open, revealing circuitry beneath. Set into this was a tiny LCD readout with a rocker switch. Currently the display showed two blinking dashes across it, separated by a dot. Maddock pressed the upper portion of the switch with a fingernail and saw numbers materialize on the display, still blinking: **10:00**. Maddock saw a tiny red button to the right of the switch and figured that was to activate the detonation countdown once the desired numbers were selected.

He looked around the ship, then decided he needed more time, but not so much that he'd be sitting around waiting for it to go off, or that Bones would get into trouble before the distraction could do any good. He hit the switch again until the numbers blinked **15:00**. Fifteen minutes should be enough time for him to place the bomb and be far enough away from it when it detonated that it would cause the needed distraction without injuring him. He knew that this single explosive was lethal, and with the correct placement it might even be able to blow a large enough hole in the ship's hull to sink it. He recalled the damage the one just like it had done to the underwater cave system.

Pondering the best place to stick it, he flipped it over and smoothed his fingers across the magnetic surface. Too close to the work deck and he could hurt Bones. Too far and it would simply take him too long to place it and then get back to Bones. At any moment the big Indian could be discovered. Or himself, for that matter, he thought, looking over his shoulder. After a moment's more reflection he decided that beneath the superstructure, as far down along the hull as he could get it would do sufficient damage, and probably not kill anyone, which he wanted to avoid if possible.

He was about to hit the red button and then paused, looking in at Shankey, who still waited patiently on his belly. No reason for this whale to be stuck in here while all Hell breaks loose. Maddock moved across the pool to the sliding gate. He reached in with the hand not holding the bomb, undid the latch and lifted the gate to reveal the opening through the hull. He ran back to the whale.

"You're free, Shankey! Go!" He patted the whale's back and pointed to the gate. The whale didn't move. "C'mon, Shankey!" The whale eyed him expectantly. Maddock brought the whistle to his lips and gave a short blast. Instantly, the pilot whale ducked beneath the water and bolted for the open gate, disappearing down the slide into the ocean. Then Maddock depressed the red button on the explosive.

He took off running. He could have waited until he got to where the bomb would be placed to set the timer, but the superstructure area was busy and he didn't want to have to sit around with his nose buried in the precision electronics if he could help it. *Fifteen minutes should be enough time...*

The ship was large and he had a fair amount of ground to cover. What's more, he had to allow for time to evade, time to find his way around. At least he felt like a real SEAL again, though, with a bomb in one hand and a gun in the other, a backup gun tucked in his waistband. Still, he hoped no one got in his way.

He ducked from one little alcove-like space to the next, at times pausing to let a crewman pass by on the walkway in front of him before continuing. He found it difficult to keep from checking his watch every thirty seconds. When four minutes had elapsed he found himself at the base of the superstructure. He craned his neck and looked up at the towering construction. He knew that most of the ship's personnel who were not already out on the work deck would be in here. He briefly considered placing the explosive somewhere inside the superstructure but then just as quickly dismissed the idea. It would likely prove fatal to at least a few people, and despite that, the many walls of the rooms there might serve to contain the explosion somewhat, limiting the physical damage to the ship.

He cast his gaze down, at the smooth curve of the hull above the waterline. If he could put the incendiary device down there, it would probably rupture the hull. Then water would flood the ship's hold, possibly the engine rooms, but he knew that a hull breach below the waterline would cause the ship to sink if the damage couldn't be repaired soon enough. Not only that, but the brunt of the explosive's damage would most likely be away from everyone on the ship, sparing them from grave injury on detonation.

But how to get down there?

He wished he had the normal complement of climbing gear SEALs normally carried and in which he was well-trained. But then, as he stared down at the black lagoon below, he had a different idea. He glanced at his watch: eight minutes elapsed, seven remaining. He heard the footfalls and voices of two people descending the stairs high above him and knew it was time to act. He could probably search about the deck for some rope or braided nylon line, but he was pretty sure that if he acted right now the simpler method would also work. *Pretty sure.*

Maddock glanced left and right to make sure no one was looking his way. Looking over the ship once more, he double-checked that the vessel was no longer moving. They were anchored in the shallow lagoon. *Good as it's going to get.*

Maddock leaped off the deck. He did his best to straighten his body during the twenty or so feet before he hit the lagoon so that he entered the water feet first, minimizing the noise from his splash. He felt the warm atoll water wash over his head, the sensation of sinking. Then, not surprisingly, he felt the crunch of sand between his toes as his feet hit the lagoon's bottom. He pushed off and knifed upward, his eyes locked on the blurry moon through shimmering the water's surface.

He emerged alongside the ship and immediately looked up along the deck rail to see if anyone had noticed the man overboard, but as far as he could tell, no one did. He looked up once at the massive, dark wall stretching up before him and kicked toward it. He would have to be very careful. Even at anchor, the ship rolled a bit with the swells and should he get too far beneath the hull, it could crush him easily, or knock him out.

He gripped the explosive in his hand as he swam up to the metal wall. It moved a little and he waited to make his move while he timed the motion.

Up...down...Up...down...Now!

Maddock stretched out the hand holding the bomb and kicked forward. He felt a panicky adrenaline surge when his hand started to arc back down through only air, thinking he had fallen short of the target in the darkness, but then he was met with a sudden, firm resistance as the hockey-puck in his hand clapped onto the ship's side...and held. He treaded water for a moment, watching the LED blink red. The bomb was holding, staying in place.

He activated the light on his watch and checked the time: *four minutes remaining.*

Maddock scissor-kicked into motion along the side of the ship toward the stern work deck. He swam underwater as much as possible to reduce the noise and chances of being seen, and because it was still a fast stroke. Even so, the ship's long body seemed to stretch out forever in front of him, almost as if it grew longer each time he surfaced for a breath. He began worry. If he was not out of the water when the explosive detonated, his body would be subject to the concussion waves. And this time he wasn't even wearing a wetsuit.

He swam faster, eyes open in the darkness, seeking the blurry form of the monstrous hull lest he stray too far out into the lagoon or even worse, stray beneath the ship. He suppressed the strong urge to stop and look at his watch. Just kept swimming like he was in a race against an invisible opponent. Before long he could hear the shouts of men and he knew he was approaching the stern work deck. He began to look for the boarding ladder.

Up ahead, still an Olympic pool length away. Again Maddock resisted the urge to check his watch and pushed on. He swam harder than he ever had in his life, even during BUDS training. Told himself not to look up, not yet, he wasn't there yet. He forced himself to count to thirty before checking his progress.

...28 Mississippi...29 Mississippi...30 Mississippi...

He raised his head, and there it was: the iron rungs set into the side of the ship, maybe fifty feet away. And just beyond that, the shadow of an airplane limned against the moonlit sky, hanging half over the rail. With Bones hopefully still undetected inside.

Maddock swam to the ladder and began to climb, his first priority to get himself out of the water where he would be much less vulnerable to the underwater explosion. When he had climbed about halfway up the side of the ship he stopped and consulted his watch, hanging there like a rock climber on the side of a huge, smooth face.

00:04...

Four seconds to detonation. Maddock braced for impact, careful not to let his body touch the ship itself, only contacting the rungs.

He closed his eyes and held his breath.

CHAPTER 31

Maddock counted down to zero and gripped the rungs on the side of the ship.

Nothing happened.

He turned his head to the right, as if to look down to where he had placed the bomb and witness an explosion so small that it hardly had any effect here. And then he felt it.

The bomb exploded, a tongue of fire bursting out of the side of the ship. He heard the muffled boom and felt the vibrations in his hands and feet as he clung to the ladder. He held on tightly, not sure how bad it would get, but after five more seconds, when the rumbling had ceased, he focused his attention upwards.

The work deck. Bones. It was time to move. He was certain the ship had been crippled, though couldn't be sure how bad the damage was at this point. Regardless, many men would be focused on responding to it, and then fixing it. This was the distraction he had sought, his opportunity to act.

Panicked shouts filled the air as Maddock monkeyed up the rungs. He slowed as he neared the top and looked to his left toward the model plane. He saw it, though not where he remembered it to be relative to his position. Either the crew had already moved it while he was gone, or else the blast must have moved it, because now it hung much lower to the water, and closer to the rungs, too. He was actually looking down into the cockpit, and...there was Bones! Still in the cockpit but now in a kneeling position, looking around.

"Bones!" Maddock called out in a strong voice that was less than a yell. He forgot about the cover name, deciding it no longer mattered. His SEAL partner still knelt in the model plane, looking about, but not back to Maddock. "Bones!" He tried again.

This time he saw Bones' head whirl.

"Over here!" Maddock waved an arm in the darkness from his position on the ladder. This time Bones locked in on the source of the sound and spotted the darkened human form hanging from the side of the ship.

"Maddock? If that's you give our ops signal." Maddock flashed a series of hand signals, almost like a gang sign, that he hoped Bones could make out well enough in the dim light.

"What happened?"

"I made up with our friend Shankey. Tell you later. We've got to get moving."

Bones looked up at the deck of the ship. "I think we *are* moving." Indeed, the ship had a pronounced list to it now, and it slowly continued to lean into the water on their side. Maddock found it hard to believe the little bomb had done that much damage, but his placement had been strategic. He looked down at the water, noting the angle. He knew that although it started slowly at first, when a ship finally did sink it happened quickly, and one did not want to be in the water with it when it did. The suction of the massive object sinking below the waves had been known to bring men down with it who were not actually trapped on the vessel. Not to mention the possibility of being crushed by the ship itself as it capsized.

"Can you get out of that plane? What've you been doing in there all this time?"

"Catching up on my sleep. Get out to where? Overboard?"

"No. Bones, it looks like this thing is going down."

"Maybe if we jump ship now and swim for the island, we'll be clear before it sinks. It's either that or we climb back aboard, but what for?"

Maddock shook his head in the darkness and pounded a fist against the steel hull. How had their mission become so derailed? It was hard to accept. So hard that he made a split-second decision, a rash one, to re-board the ship and take advantage of the chaos to make one more try for a sat-phone. That was the whole point of the explosion, anyhow.

"To make our call."

Bones was silent. They both knew that if enough time went by the Navy would come looking for them, but with the way things were going there was no guarantee they'd last that long. And an even more uncomfortable thought struck Maddock as he hung there: *would* the Navy come for them if they didn't make a call? Because no call meant that things had gone south, and if things had gone south, it might not take much for some top brass to want to wash their hands of the matter; smallpox indeed. If they did manage to make the call, on the other hand, they'd be on an aircraft bound for home in about six hours, their Amelia Earhart contraband safe and sound.

To Maddock's surprise, Bones stood up in the cockpit of the hanging replica.

"Be right there." And then he dove from the plane into the water, pushing off of the model, sending it rocking backward to swing from its cable. Maddock tensed, turning around to see where Bones landed. But Bones was a SEAL, and he gave no trace of his presence until his dark-skinned arm thrust out from the water to hook through the first rung. He began to climb, pausing once to point upward, a sign for Maddock.

Go!

Maddock started to climb, attuning his senses to the ship's deck. A lot of shouts came from farther down the ship where the damage was, but as far as he could tell the stern work deck had emptied out. Nevertheless, he stopped at the top rung and slowly raised his head until he could peer over the rail at the deck. It was empty. He looked down and saw Bones nearing his position on the ladder. He waved him on and then jumped onto the deck of the ship for the second time that night.

Bones joined him a few seconds later, both of them dripping water onto the deck. "Where to?"

Maddock pointed across the deck, over to the lifeboats they'd hidden behind earlier.

"To the superstructure, but that side's opposite where

the damage is, so we'll probably encounter less resistance if we cross here and go down that side."

Bones nodded and the two SEALs moved across the deck to the other side. They made their way forward, following the same walkway Maddock had taken earlier. The going was quicker this time, though, as they saw no signs of crew. A shrill alarm began to blare and they heard a loudspeaker announcement in Japanese. They couldn't understand it but it sounded urgent.

As they progressed, the angle of the deck grew more pronounced. It took effort not to go sliding down to their right.

"You must have done a pretty good job placing that bomb." Bones pointed to the water lapping at the base of the superstructure. This thing's going down."

Maddock eyed the oncoming rush of seawater, then looked up at the listing superstructure. "Yeah, I thought we'd have a little more time than this to look around."

"Think we can take the radio room now?" Bones gazed up at the leaning tower.

"Might as well try. Here, you get a consolation prize just for playing." Maddock removed the second K5 from his waistband and handed it to him. Bones checked the clip and reloaded it.

"Well if today's not my lucky day! Don't even tell me how you got it."

"We better hurry up." Maddock pointed to the walkway that led to the upper gangway he'd taken earlier. They encountered no resistance as they moved along. Even so, he lowered his voice to talk to Bones.

"This room up here on the right is where I saw Tomoaki interrogating Spinney and Carlson earlier."

Bones raised his K5 to the ready position as he neared the still-open door. But Maddock could no longer hear voices coming from the room and didn't think they would all be inside in complete silence. Craning his neck around the door, he saw that he was correct. The room was empty. Another door inside the room was open and led deeper into the superstructure building.

He waved Bones inside the room and they entered. They trudged across the floor at an upward angle, past the table where Spinney had sat, Maddock pointing to a smear of blood on its surface. When they reached the opposite side of the room they each waited on either side of the door. They listened a moment, the blaring siren making it difficult to discern voices, but they didn't think they heard any.

The entered a short hallway with two closed doors to their right and two to their left. All were unmarked, with no signs denoting what lay behind them, but Maddock knew the bridge would be at the front of the structure, so he motioned for Bones to go left, and they struck out in that direction. As they neared the end of the short hall they could see that the end in fact led straight to the bridge. They slowed as they approached, straining to listen.

A panicked voice. Maddock took a look into the room and was relieved to see there were only two people inside, both Japanese ship's officers. He recognized the Captain's insignia on one, and the other, talking frantically into a handheld radio, looked to be the first mate. The array of controls on the panel before them was lit up with flashing red and yellow lights. A cacophony of systems alarms brayed inside the enclosed area. The view from the expansive bridge window was terrifying, offering 180 degrees of water and burning island that made it all too clear the ship was going to capsize.

With hand signals, Maddock indicated to Bones that he would take the Captain while Bones dispatched the other officer. They moved silently into the room, weapons drawn. It occurred to Maddock that perhaps the Captain was taking action right now that could prevent the ship from sinking and that they could be about to interrupt him, but after watching for a couple of seconds it was clear that there was nothing they could do. The ship was going down. In fact, Maddock was more concerned for his safety just by being on the ship than he was being in the presence of the Mizuhi men.

But then the Captain turned around, his eyes widening as he moved to bring the radio to his lips and Maddock knew he had to act. "Drop the radio and freeze or I shoot!" He steadied the gun barrel at the Captain's chest. The radio clattered to the floor.

The first mate wasn't as compliant. He bull-rushed at Bones, charging with surprising speed for a man of such considerable bulk. But Bones was ready. He sidestepped the man, clocking him in the head with the butt of his K5 as he passed. His opponent hooked one of Bones' ankles on his way down, tripping him up. Both of them wound up on the floor, grappling while Maddock kept an extra-wary eye on the captain, warning him with his eyes not to use the fight as an excuse to try anything.

The first mate gripped Bone's gun hand and banged it against the floor. Bones head-butted him in the face, cracking his nose, which caused the man to release his grip immediately. Bones drove a fist into the man's temple, slid his arm free and rolled away, springing to his feet once he was clear. He aimed his K5 at the stunned first mate.

"Satellite phone!" Maddock shouted at the captain, who shook his head and shrugged.

"No speak."

Maddock muttered something under his breath and looked at Bones, who was staring out the window, where the view highlighted the precarious angle of the ship.

"Time to split." It concerned Maddock that Bones appeared apprehensive, since he didn't usually worry about much.

Maddock pantomimed using a phone to the captain, who again shrugged. "He's playing dumb."

"Why would he be playing dumb at this point?" Bones pointed out the window, where the water level appeared to rise by the minute. "You would think he'd want us to call someone. Anyone."

"I know you have a satellite phone," Maddock said to the captain. "The Yoshida brothers told me." At the mention of the familiar name the captain and first mate exchanged knowing glances.

Suddenly the ship tilted sharply and the man Bones had defeated slid on the floor with the sharper angle. Bones tracked him with the K5 until he came to rest on the other side of the room against the control console.

Maddock hopped over the sliding man and pounced on the captain, putting him into a control hold, one arm locked around his neck, the other bending an arm back. His gun was back in his waistband but with Bones armed he felt he could handle the captain without it.

"Take me to the satellite-phone or I break your neck!" Maddock didn't know if the man was faking his lack of English so as not to have to communicate, so for effect he applied additional pressure to the control point he had on his neck.

"Okay! I show you! Please stop."

Maddock eased up on the hold but still maintained firm control of the man, who continued talking.

"Why you want? Do no good. No help coming."

"So you do speak English."

"Little," the captain gasped in Maddock's hold.

"Take me to the phone!"

"Ship sinks! Must go!"

"After the phone!"

The roll of the ship grew even more pronounced. Even Bones took notice.

"Now or never, *Jim*." He gave Maddock a look that said he was seriously concerned for their well-being. Then he pointed outside the window to the water, where the first of the Mizuhi crew could be seen swimming for their lives away from the sinking ship and toward the flaming atoll.

"The satellite phone!" Maddock shook the captain, who pointed somewhere above his head.

"Keith, cover him." Maddock released the captain. He tried to walk to where he was pointing, but slipped and fell as the ship rolled precariously. Water splashed on the bridge windows. Maddock pushed to his feet and staggered to the section of console where the captain had pointed. Looking up he saw a closed cabinet. He reached up and opened it and saw a black plastic case.

He took it down and opened it.

"Sat-phone!"

"Charged?"

"Always the worry-wart, aren't you, Keith?"

And then the ship canted sideways until it lay nearly flat on the side where Maddock had blasted a hole.

"Let's leave these guys and get outta here! Half of this ship is underwater."

"Hold on." Maddock hit the power button on the sat-phone and grinned as it lit up. "It's got power. Thank you, captain. You and your crew are free to go. Stay out of our way and we'll leave you alone." Maddock drew his K5 and aimed it at him as if to underscore this fact.

The captain and first mate scrambled to leave, warily stumbling past Maddock and Bones and then negotiating the exit to the bridge, which now lay sideways and partially submerged. Maddock handed Bones the sat-phone and removed his backpack.

"Hold this, I need to get the number."

He removed a small address book from one of the pockets, handed it to Bones, and took the phone. "Here, read me each number from the top of the pages."

"What?"

"I wrote down the number one digit at a time, each on a separate page at the top, so in case someone gets a hold of my address book the extraction number won't be so obvious."

"I doubt this little black book has much value, knowing your lack of game with the ladies. My personal Rolodex, on the other hand, would be worth—"

"Bones! C'mon, man! We're sinking here!"

"Right. Okay, start dialling. First number: 8."

In this manner, Maddock input the entire phone number into the satellite phone. He had just entered the last digit when Bones put the book back into his pack for him and said, "Here it comes!"

A rush of water flooded into the bridge as the ship fell lower into the lagoon. Maddock held the phone up with an arm. "Still have to hit send!"

"Let's climb out of here before it floods."

But it was already too late. Both SEALs were stunned at the suddenness with which the ship succumbed to the sea once it began to flood. They realized now that it must have been flooding belowdecks the entire time they were climbing the ladder to get back aboard. Maddock held up the phone as high as he could as a new torrent of water came gushing in, threatening to sweep them off their feet.

Although he remained standing by gripping a high-backed chair in front of the console, Maddock quickly found himself submerged in water over his head. He fought to keep the phone above the inrushing deluge. He felt Bones' powerful grip steadying him, then pushing him toward the exit.

Maddock hopped up to get a breath, choking out the words, "Need to hit send!"

Bones didn't bother to reply since a new rush of water threatened to whisk them away. He managed to pull himself and Maddock through the doorway, which was now oriented sideways, confusing him as to which way was which. He didn't really care which way they were going as long as it was toward higher ground and air.

Outside the bridge they found themselves in a flooded area with ladders oriented horizontally. Bones looked around and saw a spot where they could climb on top of the superstructure's side, still awash but now the highest remaining point of the ship.

"This way, Maddock!" They swam for a ladder that they could stand on even though it lay sideways, Maddock only able to use one hand while the other held the sat-phone high. They reached the structure and Bones climbed up onto the ladder.

"It's going down, Maddock. Jump. Now!"

Bones climbed atop the wet side of the superstructure and reached back down to haul Maddock up.

"Forget me. Make the call!" Maddock held out the phone. Bones took it. He glanced at the display, saw the numbers queued up. He located the send button. Just as he brought his finger over the keypad, about to press the button, he felt a powerful swirl of water pulling around his feet as the ship went completely under.

The sat-phone display winked out as the phone covered with water a split second before Bones' finger pressed the Send button. He had time to curse once and then Bones was lifted off his feet.

CHAPTER 32

The next few seconds were a chaotic whirlwind of black rushing water, bumps and bruises, unintelligible shouts and sudden, stomach-churning drops. Every time Bones tried to kick, his feet or shins painfully collided with hard steel. He was not yet free of the ship, now totally submerged. He had no idea where Maddock was.

He pushed off something firm toward a glimmer of light. The moon. His head finally broke the surface and he started to swim toward what looked like open water. He looked down as he swam and saw the side of the ship only a few feet under. He thought maybe the ship had too much air to sink, that it was floating there, but then realized that the shallow lagoon they were in was only about thirty feet deep here, about the height of the ship.

He swam over the underwater obstruction, seeking open water. He was surprised to see many people in the water ahead of him. Saddened, too, when he realized that not all of them were still alive. He pushed past the floating corpse of a Mizuhi crewman and swam to what he thought was a safe distance beyond the shipwreck. He turned around and looked back at the sunken ship.

He didn't see Maddock. Panic welled within him as he turned in circles, looking for his friend, one question refusing to vacate his mind: *What if he didn't make it out of the ship?* He eyed the blurry form beneath him. How many of the crew didn't make it out and were entombed down there now?

He called out Maddock's name in several directions, not caring who heard. Bones had no doubt that if Maddock had made it out, he would be equally concerned about him. He looked back toward the island where the first of those who escaped from the ship were straggling onto the beach. He was sure Maddock wouldn't have gone there without locating him first. He started to swim slowly around the wreck, looking carefully, swimming close to each person he saw, even helping a couple of dazed crewmen briefly by pointing them toward shore. He didn't want to, but crossed over the sunken ship again, mindful of the protruding wreckage. He cast his eyes downward, dreading the sight of a body.

He didn't see one though, and soon he had reached the open water on the other side of the wreck. He was about to concede that there was nothing more he could do other than to swim toward shore and search for Maddock along the way when he heard a voice call out.

"Fancy meeting you here."

Bones spun around to see Maddock's face grinning at him from only a few feet away.

"Where'd you come from? Been looking all over."

"I got washed down to the far end. Took me a bit to figure out the lay of the ship underwater. Then I thought I'd see if you stuck around near where we went down."

"And to think you're okay. I could have been relaxing on the beach all this time."

Maddock glanced over at the shore. "Speaking of the beach..."

"Let's go."

"You didn't get the call off, did you?"

Bones slowly shook his head. "Phone's toast."

They began swimming across the lagoon toward shore, avoiding the more direct route crowded with survivors and skirting the long way around. They could hear many anguished cries, angry yells and just plain shouting, all in Japanese, as they traversed the lagoon.

They made good time across the calm water, not bothering with stealth since so many others were now making the same trek to shore. When Maddock could see individual palm trees on the beach he stopped swimming and let his feet hang down, rejoicing in the feel of the sandy bottom. Land. They waded ashore and sat behind a clump of palms while they watched the Mizuhi personnel make their way up onto the beach. Behind them, the island was still on fire. The scene looked like something out of a disaster movie.

Bones shook his head. "Now what? We've got no ride coming. Everybody left on this island wants to kill us. We don't even have the stuff for our objective," he finished, referencing the smallpox crate that they'd left behind in the bushes.

Maddock took off his soaked backpack and set it on the sand beside him, patting it. "At least I've still got the film. Good thing we put it in those Ziploc bags before putting it in here, though."

"So what do we do with it?"

Maddock looked out to the lagoon, where shipwreck survivors still swam ashore, then around the beach. He noted the raft they'd made, now broken apart. But it gave him an idea.

"We've got to just leave this island. However we can. On a raft, something. Anything."

Bones laughed, tossing a pebble into the water. "Even if we had something, where would we go?"

"There's an island with a resort that I saw during our flight in."

"Ronga Vanua? That's *far*, Maddock. We're talking," Bones stared out to sea as he considered it. "more like *days* instead of hours."

Maddock shrugged. "We could try to stay alive here for a few more hours until some media or authorities from the outside arrive today...if they do...but that could also end up compromising our cover. We'd be on the news, possibly detained as witnesses to what went on here. If we can leave while it's still dark."

"I guess." Bones seemed less than convinced. "But how could we leave anyway? The raft is smashed. All of the lifeboats from the ship either went down with it, never released, or they floated out to sea."

Maddock nodded. "I'm pretty sure they were never even used. But look. There's something that still floats." He pointed out into the lagoon, not far from the beach and a little to their right.

"Hey! What do you know? It's metal and it floats." Mizuhi's model Electra floated serenely on the placid water.

"It's got no engine in it weighing it down, so the sheet metal should float, especially if it's intact."

"Looks like it's going to wash right up on the beach."

They watched as it did just that, scraping across the coarse sand as it drifted onto the atoll. The two SEALs ran to it.

"Let's test it out." Maddock pushed it into knee-deep water and then hopped into the cockpit. Bones stood there and observed, watching for any signs that the craft was less than seaworthy. It seemed stable.

"Hop on in." Maddock waved an arm for him to join him in the cockpit. Bones jumped up and into the plane.

"I have to say, I've already spent quite enough time in here and wasn't really looking forward to hanging out here even more."

"What do you think? I don't see any leaks. Don't hear any water seeping in, either, do you?"

At length, Bones shook his head. "It's about as seaworthy as the old aluminum bass boat my uncle taught me to fish from on the lake. It floats, sure, but if we got into any kind of weather..." He left that unpleasant scenario unfinished before continuing on a new tack. "And there's no outboard motor on this thing. We'd have to paddle it, but it doesn't come with those, either."

"Let's get back to the beach. Maybe the raft paddles are still good."

They hopped out of the model plane and dragged it up onto the beach.

"We better hurry up and do this if we're going to," Bones said, eyeballing the growing cluster of people assembling some distance away on the beach. "At some point they might come to check out their model."

Maddock jogged over to the smashed up raft. He rummaged around in the sand for a bit and then came away with the two makeshift paddles. "At least these are intact."

Bones took them and placed them inside the model airplane. He saw a large cluster of coconuts on the ground and picked them up. "Drinking water and food." He tossed them into the cockpit as well.

"It's time to make a run for our crate." Maddock looked down the beach.

"You still have your K5?"

Maddock shook his head.

"Me neither. Got my coconut opener though." Bones patted his trusty dive knife, still sheathed on his calf.

"I lost that, too." Maddock stared ruefully at his bare leg.

"One knife between us to make this happen."

"We'll need to be stealthy."

"Not much jungle left to go through, either. It's either been burned down or still on fire."

"Hopefully those bushes where we stashed the crate haven't been burnt to a crisp. At least with the ship sinking, Mizuhi will be dealing with that instead of combing the island. Let's skirt the perimeter, this way—" Maddock pointed to their right, away from the crowd on the beach.

Bones nodded and they set out around the atoll.

CHAPTER 33

It didn't take them long to skirt the island until they approached the side where the camp was. Most of the activity was now centered on the beach, where the Mizuhi and EARHART teams alike avoided the burning jungle and discussed the aftermath of the sunken ship. When Maddock could see the camp in the distance, he pointed in the direction of the clump of vegetation where they'd hidden the crate.

"It won't be long before they organize enough to notice that we're both missing, and that a bomb ruptured the hull that caused the ship to sink, and put two and two together."

"As if they weren't looking for us already." Bones hunkered lower against the sand.

Maddock nodded. "We have got to get out of here. Let's move. We'll get that crate and come back around the same way."

He and Bones crouched low as they ran, maintaining as low a profile as possible while still being able to move fast. When they rounded the end of the island that the camp was on, they transitioned to a low-crawl, moving on their bellies across the sandy soil toward the demolished radio tent. Bones let out a muffled curse as his elbow ground into a smoldering ember.

After some more excruciating progress, Maddock scoped out the surroundings and then risked standing up for a better vantage point. He looked around quickly and then lay back down. He pointed off to their left. "Looks like our plants are still there."

"Hopefully the crate is, too."

"Let's go find out."

The two special warfare operators resumed their rapid low-crawl toward the objective. They had to skirt around a remaining pocket of wildfire that threatened to overtake their hiding place. When they rounded it, they saw no other people and had a clear path to the stand of foliage. They low-crawled the entire way, taking no chances. Smoke filled the air, lowering visibility, but down low to the ground they found it easier to breathe. They crawled directly into the grouping of plants without standing up, Maddock in the lead.

"It's here!" Maddock reached the crate and jostled it slightly, testing its weight. "Still heavy."

"We should probably open it to make sure they're still in there."

"You mean in case someone found it and took out the smallpox containers and replaced them with rocks?"

"Yeah. I'd hate to carry a box of rocks all the way back to the Commander after everything we've been through, wouldn't you?"

Maddock pulled the lid off the box and peered inside. "Still there." He replaced the lid.

"I'll get the poles." Bones slunk off deeper into the remaining greenery and came back with the two cut logs they'd used to transport the crate.

"If we use those we'll have to stand, or at least crouch," Maddock pointed out.

"We can crouch. Let's just get out of here. I'd rather be cooped up in that model airplane again with a box full of smallpox than hang around here."

"Agreed."

Maddock slid the box out from the plants while Bones took the poles and acted as lookout. After establishing that it was clear, they placed the strongbox on the poles and took up their positions at either end. They set out back the way they had come, but the going was much slower carrying the heavy box in an awkward crouch position to lower their profiles.

They forged on, though, stopping every so often to take a break where they sat low on the ground, watching and listening. On one of these breaks, they heard footsteps approaching them. A Mizuhi crewman wielding a machete hacked his way through some brush as he approached Maddock and Bones' position. Whether he was looking for them specifically, or the crates, or was simply scouting out the island, they didn't know. But they knew one thing: they had to take him out before he saw them and radioed a report.

Bones unsheathed his dive knife while Maddock slid one of the poles out from under the crate to use as a martial arts-style weapon, although it was somewhat too long. Bones stayed with the crate, guarding it, while Maddock advanced toward the approaching threat. He twirled the pole a couple of times, testing his balance with it, but decided just to go with a simple jabbing motion.

The interloper spotted him when they were about eight feet apart. He reached for his radio and raised his machete simultaneously. Maddock, in contrast, was of single-minded purpose. He thrust the pole into his opponent's abdomen. The wind left the crewman in a rush and both his radio and machete dropped to the ground.

"Bones: vines!" Bones used his knife to cut some nearby vines they could use to tie the man up. They trussed his arms and legs into a crude hog-tie. Maddock patted the man down but he carried no firearm. Then they gagged him with more vines and left him on the ground, Maddock appropriating both his machete and the radio. He made sure to turn down the volume of the radio to avoid the risk of radio chatter giving away their position as they advanced toward the beach.

With the crate loaded up again, they moved out once more, now more cautious than ever after their encounter. They pushed and pulled the crate forward on its pole system, keeping their heads down. After two more rest stops they could see the final stretch to the lagoon-front beach. It was a long haul, trundling the crate to the beach, but they made it without further incident. When they knelt on a small berm on the edge of the sand, Bones left Maddock behind with the crate to get a good look down the beach. He returned after a couple of minutes.

"Still looks about the same. Our boat-plane is still there, and the group is still hanging out on the center of the beach."

They took up the poles again, knowing that they would make a very conspicuous profile once they ventured out onto the sand where the Mizuhi group could see them.

Maddock pointed. "Let's move out along the berm until we're even with the plane, that way we'll be on the sand as little as possible."

Bones agreed and they headed off toward the plane just above the beach. They were weary from lifting the crate by now, but knew they would need one more burst of energy to make their escape. When they were looking straight across the beach at the plane, they set the poles down. Maddock addressed Bones solemnly.

"They're going to start shooting at us as soon as they see us."

"At least it's still dark out."

"Not for long." Maddock inclined his head toward the east, where the first traces of light crept over the horizon. "For this final dash I say we forget the poles, just double-carry the box to the plane, get it into the cockpit, then shove off."

"Roger that." Bones flexed his hands in preparation. The pair of SEALs hefted the crate of deadly bio-agents and tested their grip. Then it was time to go. Maddock counted them off.

"On three, two, one...now!"

They jogged off across the sand, each on one side of the weighty box, moving like a four-legged spider, turning this way and that to compensate for dips in the beach. They had just reached the plane, water lapping around their ankles, when they heard the first shouts.

"They spotted us, Bones. We better load this puppy and get while the getting's good."

A four-rung ladder led up to the cockpit. Bones, already familiar with it, climbed three steps up and turned around. Maddock pushed the deadly crate up into his outstretched arms. The weight of the crate almost pulled Bones off the ladder but Maddock shoved upward on the box and the big Indian was able to grip the edge of the cockpit and regain his balance.

"Go, Bones!" Maddock pushed on his legs to propel him over the lip of the cockpit.

Bones nearly fell into the plane, doing his level best to control the crate's descent. It landed with a thud on the bottom of the cockpit, but upright and not too hard. But there was no time to check on it now.

Someone called something in Japanese to them, followed by an English sentence: "Hey! Stop right there!"

Maddock dropped back into the shallow water and began to push the big model out into the lagoon. Just when it started to move he heard the heartbreaking sound of metal sliding on sand as the plane's landing gear caught on the bottom.

Someone yelled in Japanese.

The plane lurched sideways with the sudden shift in momentum. "What's up?" Bones called down from the cockpit. Maddock wrenched the plane free by holding onto a strut and pulling as hard as he'd ever pulled anything in his life, hoping the piece of metal didn't break free of its rivets. But it held and then the life-size model was floating free, bobbing in the gentle waves close to shore. He gave it a few more forceful shoves, and on the last one pushed off the bottom onto the ladder.

Angry yells, also in Japanese, followed, and then, as Maddock dropped into the cockpit next to Bones, the first shots came.

"Paddle, Bones. Paddle!"

They each stuck one of the handmade raft paddles over the side of the cockpit and into the water. They started to paddle, quickly falling into a familiar rhythm.

"This remind you of BUDS training or what!" Maddock looked over at Bones, who almost looked as though he were having a good time. But then a bullet pinged off of the plane, sending a spark through the darkness in front of them, and Bones grew sober, paddling even harder.

Maddock looked back and saw an angry mob standing on the beach, yelling and shaking their fists at them. He took consolation in the fact that they had no watercraft whatsoever—no lifeboats, tender vessels, not even a raft, with which to give chase. He wondered if one or some of them might try to swim after them, since they couldn't paddle faster than a good swimmer, but so far no one did. Maddock supposed he could beat them down from the boarding ladder with the paddle if they tried, but for now it seemed they were content to take potshots at them from the comfort of the beach.

A round penetrated the fuselage, luckily above the waterline, but Maddock knew that they needed to put more distance between themselves and the island. He paddled harder than he ever had in his life, even in the grueling SEAL training exercises they'd been put through in San Diego, eyes fixed on the line of frothing water that marked the outer edge of the lagoon.

They passed over the sunken ship, its gloomy form now a permanent fixture of the underwater landscape. Random floating objects still trickling out of the wreck bobbed in their wake as they rowed hard for the outer reef. One more shot zinged against the plane's tail fin, and after that the shots petered out, the men on the beach realizing that the impromptu rowboat was too far away to hit.

Then a new problem presented itself: maneuvering through the narrow cut in the reef out to the open ocean. But it was one they much preferred to being shot at. Still, they both knew that should they miscalculate and wind up on the shallow rocks, their fragile craft would be dashed apart, and they would have no choice but to return to the atoll like a pair of wet dogs climbing out of a pool.

"Right turn," Bones called out as they approached the opening in the reef. Maddock lifted his paddle from the water while Bones dug his in, and the cumbersome model swung to the right.

"Straight ahead!" Bones relished his role as rowing

captain; he'd been a leader in that area back in BUDS, and he called out directions with gusto, leaning into his paddle strokes, giving it everything he had. Maddock knew that he somehow had a good sense for how to control the ungainly craft, and he followed orders, doing his best to keep them off the reef. And then they were shooting through the cut, flying into open ocean, the breakers spraying off the sides of their boat-plane that had just delivered them from the atoll.

"We made it!" Bones yelled. He turned around to look back at the distant beach. "Screw you guys!"

Maddock stared at his friend, resting. Bones saw that Maddock wasn't sharing in his enthusiasm.

"Now what?"

"Do you know where we're going, Bones?"

The burly Cherokee stared out to sea, at the largest body of water on the planet, the Pacific Ocean. "I guess not."

Maddock reached into his backpack and brought out the digital camera. He activated the screen while they floated there, just beyond the reef. He scrolled through the images he'd taken, seeking the ones he'd snapped during their helicopter flight in.

"Here." He held the camera's small screen so Bones could see it. "This is the nearest island to here that had any kind of civilization on it."

Bones squinted at the picture, which showed a white sandy beach fringed with palm trees, with a row of over-water bungalows stretching out over an aquamarine lagoon. "Oh, I remember that. But geez, Maddock, by helo that place was like ten or fifteen minutes away....in this thing it could take...days."

"Then we better start rowing."

Bones looked out to sea. "Which way?"

Maddock oriented them with the photograph, pointing off into the distance. Bones looked up at the sky and fixed their position against the rapidly fading stars. "I learned celestial navigation as a kid to honor my ancestors. It's getting light out now but I can fix our position by the stars to get underway on the right course and then hopefully it won't be cloudy when the sun comes out and I can use that."

"Well then—hey, look!" Maddock pointed off to their right, where a sleek, dark shape moved slowly along the surface.

"You've got to be kidding me." Bones slapped his forehead. "Shankey! We can't take any hits in this thing, Maddock, if he—"

"Hold up, look. He's not coming at us." The pilot whale stopped and spyhopped, sticking its head vertically out of the water. It looked at Maddock and Bones, made some clicking noises, then turned and swam off in the opposite direction.

"He's not going to attack us? No freaking way!"

"Nope. Just wanted to say thanks for getting him out of that tank, I guess."

Bones called after the whale. "Later, dude. Hope you find yourself a hot porpoise babe or two."

Laughing, the two SEALs paddled out to sea, the sun rising off to their right.

CHAPTER 34

Two days later

"I never want to look at another coconut as long as I live. No pina coladas, either." Bones stepped from the model Electra onto the sun-dappled, sandy bottom in front of a picturesque, palm-studded beach. "Well, maybe a pina colada. I'm not an unreasonable man."

Maddock eased the old crate down to him and then got out next, wearing his backpack and splashing into the waist-deep water. They hauled the heavy crate to shore and laid in the soft sand.

"Check it out." Bones pointed at a cluster of grass huts off to their left. "Where there's grass huts, there might be scantily-clad ladies."

"Hold up. We should do something with our trusty steed here."

"Do something with it? Like what?"

Maddock shrugged. "It'll attract a lot of attention if we just leave it here. We should sink it."

"Sink it?" Bones hefted the crate.

"Yeah, just rip a hole in the bottom and sink it right here, so it's out of sight and probably won't be found by anybody until after we've left."

"Good idea. It'll keep the historians busy, too, whenever it's finally found and they say, 'Hey, look. It's an old Electra! Must be Amelia Earhart's!'"

Maddock grinned. "Let's get her out to deeper water and sink her." He ignored Bones' grumbling as they took Electra away from shore.

"Mind if I do the honors?" Bones asked. "I've got my coconut opener right here." He unsheathed his dive knife and gashed a hole in the plane's thin, sheet metal side just below the water line. He ripped another gash and then another. A few more hacks and water began filling the craft.

They watched as the plane settled lower in the water, then swam back to the beach where Bones kissed the sand for dramatic effect.

When Maddock looked back at the plane, it was almost entirely submerged.

"No way am I lugging this damn thing all the way over there." Bones prodded the crate with his toe and cast a tired glance down the beach toward the cluster of buildings.

Maddock pointed at some scrub brush at the top of the beach. "We can hide it here until it's time to go." They obscured the crate under the brush and then set off down the beach. At the far end they saw sunbathers lying out on lounge chairs, even a couple of kids playing ball. They took a manicured path up off the beach through a landscaped area to a thatched hut. A faded wooden sign reading "Tiki Bar" hung from the thatched roof.

"Score!" Bones looked the happiest Maddock had ever seen him. An elderly gentleman of Pacific Island descent tended bar for a smattering of customers, but there were plenty of open seats. Maddock and Bones, shirtless and shoeless and more than a little sunburned after their marathon open water paddle, didn't look all that out of place as they took two barstools. Maddock thought the bartender might question whether they were staying here, but he simply asked if he could get them something to drink. He told them that he was running a special on coconut rum drinks and Bones grimaced.

Both of them ordered waters, draft beers and meals of fried fish. As they drank the delightfully cold beverages, Bones lowered his voice and said to Maddock, "You have any cash in that backpack?"

Maddock frowned and scratched his head. "Let me think. I've got a digital camera, my address book, and a bunch of old pictures that Amelia Earhart took."

Bones nodded and took another sip from his beer. "So how are we going to pay for this?"

Maddock grinned. "Oh yeah, and a little spare cash. Drinks are on me."

"Did I ever tell you you're my best friend?" Bones raised his beer in salute.

Maddock took the address book from his pack and opened it. "But if we're lucky, we can get Uncle Sam to pay."

He asked the bartender if he could use the telephone, having no idea if there was one. The man smiled and brought out an old, corded, push-button phone from under the bar and set it in front of Maddock before turning back to another customer. Maddock lifted the handset from the cradle and put an ear to it. He nodded. Dial tone. He consulted his book and placed the call to the encrypted military line.

Maddock grinned as he pressed the buttons, entering the code to access the military satellite network. They both knew it was not that simple, of course. The pickup had been carefully prearranged and discussed during the military helicopter flight from the destroyer en route to San Diego International. From the time they made the call, a complex chain reaction of logistical events would be put into action that culminated in an unmarked, high-speed, long-range helicopter landing on the beach approximately six hours later.

Maddock put the phone to his ear as a series of clicks and beeps indicated the connection was being made. Then he listened to an automated message.

"Your request has been received and position noted. Standby for extraction." The line went dead.

Maddock looked at Bones. "They're on their way."

Maddock saw the Cherokee grinning while he looked at a small piece of paper he held between two fingers.

"What is that?"

Bones smiled while he looked at the tiny square. "Something I found in the cave that somehow survived in my pocket."

He handed it to Maddock, who took a close look at it while they sipped from their beers at the tiki bar.

It was a cancelled postage stamp from Lae, New

Guinea. Date: July 1, 1937.

EPILOGUE

One week later

Commander Roberts almost wished he hadn't seen the prints that were made from the exposed but undeveloped film his two SEALs had brought back from the island. They had done one hell of a job, he had to admit. Be that as it may, he wished the whole mess would just go away, and he believed it would now that this whole thing was over.

He walked with the Records Clerk in a humongous, hangar-like building between massive stacks of warehoused objects, files, articles and reports from classified cases spanning decades' worth of administrations. He could have delegated this task but he wanted to personally make sure that it was done right. The clerk made a left turn down another three-story-high stack and Roberts followed close behind.

For all the sensationalism of the EARHART group's press conferences, media blitzes, and threats of lawsuits against the Mizuhi Development Corporation, they had been able to produce very little in the way of solid proof that they had discovered the final resting place of Amelia Earhart. Visitors to the island coming to investigate Spinney's claims had left underwhelmed. They had no airplane. No significant artifacts. Only an ecologically compromised island and a lot of finger-pointing between them and Mizuhi, who had filed a lawsuit of their own in a Honolulu circuit court against Fred Spinney's group claiming extensive property damage.

Roberts shook his head as he recalled the most haunting of the black-and-white photographs to come out of the film his SEALs had recovered.

It was a shot taken from inside the rear cargo area of what had been verified to be a Lockheed Electra 12 airplane. The image depicted Amelia Earhart in the pilot's seat, her head facing to the right. In the co-pilot's seat, a Japanese solider, his face locked in a determined grimace, aimed a pistol at her.

"Commander? Are you all right?"

Roberts shook himself from his reverie. The clerk had stopped in front of a towering stack.

"Yes, I'm fine. So this is where it goes?"

"Yes, sir. I'll take it up." The clerk stepped onto a mechanized lift necessary to reach the higher shelves.

Roberts took one last look at the sealed envelope containing the negatives and handed it over. The clerk pressed a button on the lift and up he went into the stacks; ten feet…twenty feet high, then placed the envelope on a shelf between many, many more, stretching out almost endlessly to either side of them.

The commander wondered if anyone would ever lay eyes on the material again. He certainly couldn't be sure of it. Now that they had the smallpox safely secured in a Level Four biosafety facility, there wasn't really a need to revisit it.

Amelia Earhart's Electra had been lost again.

THE END

ABOUT THE AUTHORS

David Wood is the author of the popular action-adventure series, The Dane Maddock Adventures, as well as several stand-alone works and two series for young adults. Under his David Debord pen name he is the author of the Absent Gods fantasy series. When not writing, he co-hosts the Authorcast podcast. David and his family live in Santa Fe, New Mexico. Visit him online at www.davidwoodweb.com.

Rick Chesler is the author of the popular Tara Shores Thriller series and several other thrillers. Rick holds a Bachelor of Science in marine biology and has had a life-long interest in the ocean, its creatures and the people who call it their home. When not at work as a research project manager, he can be found scuba diving or traveling to research his next thriller idea. He currently lives in the Florida Keys with his wife and son. Visit him online at rickchesler.com.

Made in the USA
San Bernardino, CA
05 May 2015